D1338071

Lachlan cursed this ridiculous farce.

More than twenty years of selfless service to the King, repaid by the fetter of marriage to a woman who was scared of her own shadow. If it wasn't so permanent he might have laughed. Indeed, he had seen the puzzled faces of his men as they tried to fathom out the character of his new wife and failed.

She had hit him!

His frightened mouse of a wife had hit him. Hard. And in the shadowed depths of her amber eyes he had recognised what he so often saw in his own.

Secrets.

Sophia James lives in a big old house in Chelsea Bay on Auckland's North Shore, with her husband, who is an artist, three kids, two cats, a turtle and a guide dog puppy. Life is busy because, as well as teaching adults English at the local Migrant School, she helps her husband take art tours to Italy and France each September. Sophia has a degree in English and History from Auckland University, and she believes her love of writing was formed reading Georgette Heyer, with her twin sister, on the porch of her grandmother's house, overlooking the sandhills of Raglan.

Previous novels by Sophia James:

FALLEN ANGEL
ASHBLANE'S LADY
HIGH SEAS TO HIGH SOCIETY
MASQUERADING MISTRESS

KNIGHT OF GRACE

Sophia James

MILLS & BOON®

Pure reading pleasure™

First published in Great Britain 2008
Harlequin Mills & Boon Limited,
Eton House, 18-24 Paradise Road, Richmond, Surrey TW9 1SR

© Sophia James 2008

ISBN: 978 0 263 20221 2

Set in Times Roman 13 on 16 pt.
08-1208-62044

Printed and bound in Great Britain
by CPI Antony Rowe, Chippenham, Wiltshire

KNIGHT
OF GRACE

It is 1360 and Scotland is in chaos. King David has just returned to Edinburgh after eleven years of captivity under the English and the vacuum of power created in his absence brings a crisis. While some landowners want to retain their hard-won sovereignty, others side with the English and the claims of those disinherited under Robert Bruce. Border politics is murky, and David himself makes things more difficult when he thinks to cede his crown to the Duke of Clarence, Edward of England's son. A few honourable men support the concept of a self-determining Scotland, based on the principles of freedom written in the Declaration of Arbroath.

Laird Lachlan Kerr is one of these men…

…we will never on any conditions be subjected to the Lordship of the English. For we fight not for glory, nor riches, nor honours, but for freedom alone, which no good man gives up except with his life.

Words from the Declaration of Arbroath, April 1320, and affixed with the seals of forty Scottish nobles.

Chapter One

August 1360—Grantley Manor, Clenmell, Durham, England.

Lady Grace Stanton watched the man walking towards her. Tall, dark and *beautiful*.

She had not expected that.

This beauty worried her more than the danger that cloaked him or the distance he wore like a mantle, and when he finally stood before them and the dust of the horses had settled, she schooled her expression and looked up.

He was disappointed. She could see it in his eyes. Pale shadow blue with suspicion simmering just below the surface. Her heart sank and she felt the aching cold of his distrust. With a feigned smile she took his offered fingers into her own, hating her bitten-down nails and the way the red dryness on her skin looked against the brown smoothness of his.

She had been burdened with this complaint for the whole of her twenty-six years. But today at least the skin beneath her eyes was not crusty raw and weeping.

'Lady Grace.' He relinquished contact as soon as he had said her name.

'Kerr.' Her uncle was the Earl of Carrick and his tone was anything but welcoming, his furrowed gaze including the twenty or so clansmen who sat on horses behind Kerr. 'We expected you a week ago.'

'Ye have the priest, then?' Kerr cut in, dispensing completely with any pretence to manners.

'We do. Father O'Brian has come up from—"

'Then bring him here.'

'But my niece is not even dressed.'

'A dress is the least of her worries given the decree of my king.' His words were flat. Insolent, almost. Teetering on the edge of treason. As Grace looked around at her uncle, the harshness of light made him seem old; a man who had outgrown the demands of battle and wanted now to amble towards his dotage with some semblance of peace. When her glance fell on the weaponry that the Kerrs bristled with, she knew more plainly than ever before the true price of politics. One false move and her family would suffer, for innocent pawns were easily expendable against a background of political frustration.

'I th-th-think, U-Uncle, that you should ask F-F-Father O'Brian to c-c-come out to us.' Lord. Her stammer was far worse than it usually was. Grace heard rather than saw the way the men behind Kerr murmured and her pulse quickened so markedly that she wondered if she would fall over from a lack of breath.

No, she would not!

Biting down on her bottom lip, she was very still, centring calm across panic until she felt the alarm recede.

'You would be married here? Outside? But you had hoped…'

'Nay, Uncle. Here will be g-good.'

Hopes! She scanned the face of the warrior opposite, fully expecting mirth or at the very least pity, but saw neither.

Just a duty, she suddenly thought. This marriage was a duty, a way of appeasing his monarch and filling the coffers of his own keep.

'Tainted with a skin condition, but with good child-bearing hips.' The envoy from Edward the Third of England had uttered exactly those words as she had been summoned for the first time before him. She remembered her uncle's momentary fury as the decree was laid in his hands, a piece of paper that would change their lives for ever. If he did not comply, Grantley Manor would be at risk. Grantley! The family seat lost if not for the sacrifice of marrying a plain and ageing niece off to a chosen spouse. Even her uncle had limits as to what he was prepared to lose.

The will of kings. A union forged while all grappled with the concept of the self-determination of Scotland.

She could see the outline of impatience in Lachlan Kerr's eyes, sky blue see-through-you eyes with just a hint of grey. Eyes that said he surely knew the extent of her reputation at court, where the rumours of who she was and wasn't were touted in the songs of unkind jesters; a figure of fun to give the ladies and lords a moment's respite against the harsher realities of intrigue. Stephen had told her last summer, after he had returned from London, her cousin reciting the faults, thinking he did her a favour with the warning.

Perhaps he did, Grace mused. A year ago she might have missed the censure and pity so plainly etched on Kerr's face and imagined it merely as nerves. Today the full shape of an undisguised gall was evident in his frown, in his stance and in the way he stood before them, one hand on his hip and the other on the hilt of a sword.

His brother's seconds!

This was not his choice, not his want. She pulled the sleeves of her dress down lower, glad when the lace covered even the very tips of her fingers.

A movement from the front door drew everyone's attention as Judith, Anne and Ginny bustled down the stairs towards them, their fair hair burnished gold by the sun. Individually her young cousins were pretty; together they were much more than that. She felt the interest of the men behind Kerr as a sharpening of awareness, a distinct and utter masculine appreciation. She refrained from seeing if her husband-to-be was watching them in the same way, reasoning that even a slim shadow of doubt was preferable to the knowing of it.

Judith leaned over to her and whispered exactly what it was Grace was thinking. 'He is far bigger than we had thought.' Her husky lisp contained both tremor and question.

Nerves, Grace decided and squeezed the hand that threaded through her own, trying to give some sort of reassurance. Anne and Ginny crowded in behind. Waiting. She felt their collected fear like an ache and gestured them back, behind her, where she could stand between any threat of violence, should it come from the Scots.

'These are m-my cousins.' She felt she had to say something as an awkward silence hung across the group and was pleased when her uncle tried to ease the tension.

'The envoy led us to believe that you would be at Grantley before the last Sabbath, Laird Kerr.'

'I was…detained.'

Detained. The word held an edge of dark despair.

By what? By whom?

A woman, perhaps? The thought slipped into Grace's mind as she observed him, for he had been married before. She knew, because Judith had overheard the king's man saying so to his travelling companion, just before he had spoken of the lack of coinage the Kerrs were cursed with, and the desperate need of the Laird to find a woman of means.

Means. Indeed she had that.

With a substantial inheritance and a bloodline that was the very zenith of pure, her dowry would go far to help the ailing finances of any family down on its luck.

Marriage! Would this stranger demand his conjugal rights this very evening in front of his band of men? Lord, even the idea of removing her clothes had the blood rushing to her cheeks.

He would see.

He would know.

He would understand the truth of what before had only been whispered at and if he thought her ugly now… She shook her head. Hard. And feeling the sharp ends of Anne's nails digging into the flesh of her inner arm, she tried to take charge.

'W-Would you c-come inside and have a meal?'

Better, she thought. Much better. At least every word was not cursed with a stammer. Raising her glance, she looked straight at the man who would be her husband. In the direct sunlight he had squinted his eyes and the gathering lines to each side of his face were…attractive. No other way to describe them. Much more attractive than his brother had been, and he was deemed a handsome man! Angry at her wayward musings, she spoke again.

'Father O'B-Brian is still at prayer and could be so for a while. If you could p-p-poss-poss…'

He stopped her simply by laying his hand across her own and she had the distinct impression of help.

Help?

Confused, she looked around. Judith's eyes were filled with tears and weepy, and Anne and Ginny's faces were pale. Lord, she prayed her cousins would not burst forth into noisy wailing. Not in front of these men. Not when the safety of Grantley depended on a marriage, signed, sealed and delivered.

Sacrifice. Expediency. Words that had shaped her life for all her years and would now continue doing so. It was written in the blood of men and in the ink of kings.

Irrevocable. Unalterable. Settled.

There could be no going back or refusal. Her life for her family's lands.

She imagined herself with a sword in hand, beating back

any enemy, protecting them with her finesse, winning a battle that no other ever could have...

The thought was so ridiculous she began to smile, but caught back the humour as flinted steeled eyes met her own. And swallowed. Now was not the time for foolish flights of fancy.

'My uncle has some f-fine Rhenish wine.'

When Kerr inclined his head and gestured to his men, she felt a sigh of relief. Not quite time to leave, then. Still an hour or so before she would be wrenched from here and transplanted to Belridden, his keep a good forty miles to the north.

With a heavy heart she led the men in and, conscious of the fact that the Laird of Kerr walked directly behind her, tried her hardest to minimise her limp.

Following Lady Grace, Lachlan decided that her hair beneath the ugly skullcap was long and red. Not the quiet red of auburn or the burnished red of copper, her hair was a bright gilt shade that showed up in her brows and on the freckles that her cheeks were blemished with. And the skin on both her arms was strangely marred by dryness.

She was not at all the girl he had expected. Nay, woman, he corrected himself, for he knew her to be twenty-six. Long past the more usual time of marriage, long past the silly vacuous age of rising hope. For that at least he was glad. He frowned as he remembered back to the things that were said of Lady Grace Stanton.

Frightened. Temperate. Plain. A dreamer. Aye, and for these things she would do. And do well.

No temptress to dole out her favours to other men when he was away from the Kerr land. No competition to Rebecca, either; with the quick tongue of his mistress silenced, he knew that life at Belridden would be much easier than if he had brought home a beauty.

Lady Grace would suit him admirably. A homely and well-dowered wife. A woman who would not complain. A lady who would have the means to run his castle and the hips to bear his children. It was enough, and, if life had taught him anything, it had been not to expect too much.

The flash of humour as she had tempted him with the wine had been worrying, though! He had seen that look before in the eyes of experienced courtesans. A certain arrogance and self-assurance that came with the innate confidence of beautiful women.

Grace Stanton was hardly beautiful.

And yet she was not ugly either. Not when the sun hit the light velvet of her eyes or shadowed deep dimples on each cheek. Not when her fingers had touched his arm and he had felt something more than mere indifference.

Frowning he glanced over at the younger cousins. Frail, fragile and fearful.

She protected them, supported them, held their shaking fingers in her own and shepherded them inside, like a mother hen might do to her chicks when the rowdy farmyard dog was nigh.

He looked at his men and saw that their interest was firmly placed on his wife-to-be, and on the ring she wore.

He had seen it immediately when first he had taken her hand.

His brother's ring.

The gold insignia burnished by time.

Ten months since Malcolm had been killed in an accident at Grantley with the explanations of his demise as patently false as the proffered sympathy. No body had ever been found, the ravine he had fallen into deep and craggy and a river at its bottom channelling out to sea. Lach's brows drew together as he remembered the Earl of Carrick's oldest son Stephen giving his grandmother and him a version of the death with lying eyes and a shaking voice. Fallen during a ride after giving his troth to Stephen's cousin? Looking at the lady herself, Lach could not believe her to have inspired a proposal from a brother who had courted and left many of the beauties of both England and Scotland.

Curtailed by politics, however, any revenge was compromised by the unchangeable declaration of meddlesome kings.

A wife of means would be provided to pacify the Kerr clan for the loss of their kin. One brother for another and half of the spoils of the Stanton dowry to fill the empty coffers of Belridden. A quarter would go to Edward; a sop perhaps for Lionel, the Duke of Clarence, in his own bid for the Scottish throne, and the rest to David, a welcome windfall with the merks of the Berwick Treaty largely unpaid. When Lachlan had protested against the offer, it was made clear to him by David that he had no choice. Marry the girl or risk his lands! Put so succinctly, he had packed his things and headed south to get her: his brother's intended, the Kerr ring still on her finger carved in gold and rubies. Unhidden.

The bile rose in his throat. Had it just been he, he might well have laid his hands around the slim column of her neck and squeezed the truth from her about what had happened to his brother.

But he couldn't. Not with the fate of his people resting so firmly in her traitorous palms. Not with the threat of winter looming, close and long, and a hundred clan children who would not see the next spring should he take unwise retribution.

He hated the feeling of helpless anger he was suddenly consumed with. Hated the knowing smile on Grace Stanton's face and the muted sobs of the group of yellow-haired girls. Hated Grantley and its luxury. Hated the problem of poverty he was faced with, and no way short of marriage and a rich wife to solve it.

When the front doors were opened by myriad servants, the opulence of the manor made him stop. The whole of the bottom floor of Belridden would have fitted into this one single salon, wealth screaming from each priceless piece of furniture. He wondered what Grace Stanton would make of the hall at his keep and knew the answer with a sinking heart. She would probably have one peek and burst into tears and take to her bed for a week. Wasn't that the way of wealthy women?

Her bed. His bed? Their bed? Lord, he had not even had the time to think through the sleeping arrangements before being summoned south on the orders of his king. A niggling worm of doubt turned inside him.

To bed her?

To unpeel the high-necked gown from her body and discover the woman underneath. To enter her with the legality of the king's missive between them and produce an heir? To see her stomach full swelled with the seed of his loins, ripe, womanly, available.

Even with his brother's band on her finger, the idea was not repugnant. Not repelling. Nay, the very idea took on a breathless possibility and shimmered between them as they took their seats at the table.

Sensual. Shocking. Raw.

He noticed how she slid her chair as far away from him as she could manage.

'S-S-Stephen will be here t-t-tomorrow.'

Her stutter made her strangely vulnerable and as their eyes caught close he saw something in them that garnered his pity. Pure and utter effort marked the velvet, and a light sweat beaded her upper lip.

'We will be gone long before then, aye.' No point in pretending otherwise. He was annoyed with his sudden want to make things a little easier for her. Annoyed, too, when the softness that had been in her eyes sharpened and she turned away.

A wife to provide a suitable heir. That was all he needed.

That and her sizeable dowry.

And as soon as he could rip Malcolm's ring from her finger, he would.

Chapter Two

The party from Belridden hardly ate a thing.

They hardly touched the fowl or pork or salmon that appeared in course after course from the generous kitchens of Grantley. Nay, they sat there like a sullen solid wall of plaid and muscle and helped themselves to wine. But that was all.

Did they think the fare poisoned? Or was it food so unlike the nourishment at Belridden that they just could not steel themselves to try it?

A headache that had begun outside blossomed and the zigzagged beads of light that tore through Grace's vision widened. She would be married under the name of God to a man she would only be able to half-see.

Blinking hard, she caught his glance.

No, his half-glance. One eye, no nose and the glimmer of a neck, and the rest of his body disappearing into jagged nothingness.

Wiping wet hair from her forehead, she no longer cared about the welts of thickened skin hidden beneath her fringe as she counted slowly backwards from one hundred. Sometimes that helped. Today it didn't.

The arrival of Father O'Brian lifted the silence, his lilting accent welcomed.

'I had it from the cottagers that the Kerr party were here, Lady Grace, and wondered when you'd be having a need of my services?'

He stopped as he came fully into the room and stared at the strangers opposite. She'd always thought Patrick O'Brian a large man, but compared to Lachlan Kerr he suddenly looked small. Still, to give him his due, the cleric tried to stand his ground as his eyes slid across the numerous swords. 'I cannot marry you in battle gear, Laird Kerr. In the face of our Lord such a thing would be sacrilege.'

'Then you cannae marry me at all,' Kerr returned, no waver in his voice, just a cold, hard certainty. 'And when ye don't comply with the demands of your liege, the way forward from here for you might well be an uneasy one.'

Her uncle began to splutter, a red sheen covering his cheeks. Grace could see it because she had massaged the tight muscles in the back of her neck for the past two minutes and felt the instantaneous relief to the pain behind her eyes. As if by magic the spots of jagged light disappeared to be replaced by a headache. Dull. Heavy. Constant.

But she could see. See Lachlan Kerr's anger and the gritted teeth of his twenty men. See the pale faces of her cousins and the nervous demeanour of both the priest and her uncle.

And in that moment Grace knew that, unless she took

charge of this farce, everyone in her family would be at risk. More than at risk. Death lurked easy when one disobeyed the commands of the king, and her uncle's building rage worried her the most.

'I am certain that G-God's will would not be slighted.'

Lord, if the Laird of Kerr were to walk out now she doubted the aged priest's superiors would be easy on him for making such a mistake and the token of this truce to secure a fragile peace would be trampled beneath the weight of error.

Her cousins. Her uncle. Grantley.

In danger.

There was only one thing to do.

'I w-wish to be m-married, now.'

Judith burst into tears and knocked over her wine, the red blush of it staining the tablecloth, a wider and wider blot along the pristine fold of linen. A sign? A portent? Was history repeated in such a simple action? The weight of uncertainty in Ginny's eyes deepened and the smooth cold gold of Malcolm Kerr's ring bound the past with the present.

Fickle and faithless and laughing, the secret of his death lay in the room like a shout, like a screaming echo of unrightness, like a shroud of shame that had brought them all to this pass, this penance.

Father O'Brian trembled against the lintel of the door, his fingers clutching the cross at his neck whilst he uttered a prayer, the dull monotones reflecting the mood as her uncle turned an even deeper shade of red.

Her wedding hour.

Chaos.

Her dress hanging in the corner of her cupboard, shrouded in calico. Unworn.

The flowers she had imagined to fashion into a fragrant bouquet, unpicked.

And a would-be husband that looked at her in the manner of a man who did not care at all.

'He will take my hand and stare into my eyes and a single tear will run down his handsome cheek as he tells me how much he loves me, adores me, cannot live without me, his finger softly tracing the smile on my face...'

Grace shook her head. How often had she told her cousins this story as she lay beside them in the hours before wakefulness became slumber, dreamtime cameos where knights of honour and chivalry and faithfulness rode into Grantley demanding love. Her love, despite the itchy rash and cursed stutter. In these stories she had none of them. Even her hair was a less fiery shade of red.

Dreams?

Reality!

When Kerr dragged her into the space beside him, his hands were neither soft nor careful. When he demanded that the priest give the oath to bind them together, she heard hatred rather than love.

And when he gave her his answer two words kept repeating again and again in her head.

For ever. For ever. For ever.

A warm wash of horror flooded through her as, before God and her family as witnesses, she was married. For ever. Sealed in the eyes of the Lord and the law with an unbreakable and eternal promise.

When it was finished and her husband handed her a large goblet of wine, she drank it without taking breath and then helped herself to another, her more normal sense of optimism submerged under the heavy weight of duty.

Judith held her hand, hard clasped and shaking.

'If he is anything like his brother, Grace…'

She did not let her finish. 'He w-won't be.'

'You can tell?'

'I can hope.'

'We could be at Belridden in two days to get you if you needed to come home.'

'I am married n-now, Judith. Under what law should I be able to leave my h-husband?'

They looked at each other in silence, the enormity of everything a dark shadow of truth in both their eyes.

'This should not have been your cross to bear. It should have been mine. I am Ginny's sister, after all; if anyone had to pay the price for Malcolm Kerr's death, it should have been me.'

Grace looked at her new husband, their eyes meeting across the crowded room. He was as beautiful as she was plain, the pale blueness of his eyes catching her anew with the contrast of colour against his darkness of hair.

David's knight. A man who had ruled the fields of battle from France to Scotland for a decade. She had heard the tales from various bards when they had come to Grantley with their songs and their stories. Sword, scabbard, mail and shield: Lachlan Kerr's weapons of choice as he rode beneath the gold-and-red standard of the lion of Scotland, its border pierced by ten fleurs-de-lis.

And now her husband.

She turned his ring around the third finger on her left hand and the warmth of the metal made her smile.

A sign. Of hope? She wondered about her marriage night, about being close to such a man.

'If you l-love me, Judith, you will promise to st-stay silent about everything, because if you do not then all of this will have been in vain.'

Judith did not look happy at all. 'Perhaps if you told him about what he tried to do to Ginny…'

'And ruin her r-reputation for ever?'

'This is for ever too, Grace.'

'I know, but I am twenty-six and Ginny is b-barely sixteen.'

'She has not spoken since…' Judith stopped and re-grouped. 'Perhaps she never will.'

'T-ten months is only a l-little time. With c-care…'

A single tear traced its way down Judith's cheek. 'You were always the best and the bravest of us, Grace, and if Lachlan Kerr ever hurts you even a little…'

'He won't.'

'You are certain?'

The pale stare of her husband caught her across the head of her cousin, beckoning her, arrogance written in every line of his face.

Grace tipped up the goblet she held and finished the draught within. This charade was for a reason and their marriage was final. There could be no going back on such a promise even had she wanted to.

'I am c-certain,' she returned before limping over to join him.

He barely acknowledged her as she came to stand beside him, his shoulders a good foot above her own even when she straightened. He spoke to his men of his hopes for Scotland and of his want to be again in the land of his birth before another moon waned.

So soon? He would not stay here at Grantley for one night? The shock of such an imminent departure made her breathing uneven and she felt his gaze full upon her.

'Belridden has favours that Grantley lacks. The mountains around it, for example, are lauded for their bounty when hunting.'

Grace tried to smile, tried to understand that it was a reassurance he gave her. Bounty in hunting? All she could see in her mind's eye was a far-off, lonely place with trails and tracks used for forage and pursuit.

The easy luxury of Grantley closed in. 'I have n-no knowledge of h-hunting, Laird K-Kerr,' she returned and the red-haired man next to him laughed.

Lachlan Kerr did not, however, his eyes bruised with the growing realisation of the enormous gulf that lay between them as he wiped his mouth free of wine on his sleeve before turning.

'It is time to go.'

Even his men on the other side of the room heard his words, standing almost as one, and the colourful gowns of her cousins seemed caught in a time frame, like an etching, England swallowed up by the muted earthy tones of plaid. Judith's wail came first as she pushed forwards, her arms encircling Grace, tears running freely down her cheeks.

'I cannot bear to think of life without you, Grace,' she cried, 'the stories you tell us will be so sorely missed.'

Grace noticed the look of interest that flinted across Lachlan Kerr's face.

'Stories?'

'Grace has the most wonderful imagination. She tells us tales at night.' Bright red coated Judith's cheeks as she registered the Laird's attention.

'I am c-certain that I sh-shall b-be back often.' Her own reassurance vacillated as incredulity appeared on the face of every Scotsman. The sheer volume of wine she had consumed began to take effect, for she rarely drank very much. The room tilted and the noise in it dimmed as she felt her hand on Judith's arm without any sense of it really being there. The goodbyes to her other cousins and to her uncle were just as unreal, the farewells far away through the haze of unreality and less difficult than they would have been were she sober.

A kiss and a hug, food pressed into her hands and her cape draped around her and then the party was outside and she was up, on a horse in front of her new husband. A hastily packed chest on a steed behind. Quick steps to another life, the angst of it all banished by too many glasses of fine Rhenish wine.

She wiped her eyes and struggled for control, for normality, but already the whirling tiredness was upon her. Leaning back against the solid warmth was comforting and she did not push away the arm that anchored her firmly into place.

The landscape swam out of focus, soft, troubled. Almost known.

'Keep still.' The voice was angry-close and as her eyes flew open wide the world again began to settle.

They were in the foothills of the Three Stone Burn, miles from Grantley.

And heading north.

Away from home. Away from her cousins and her uncle and the people she had known all her life.

She wriggled forwards, her muscles tight from the effort of countering the pressure from the easy canter of his horse.

His horse!

She was on his horse. Hot panic and cold fear.

'Get me off…let me down… I want to get down…' When she flung herself away the ground came up, fast, and hit her hard against the shoulder, winding her.

She had not been on a horse since… She shook her head and tried not to remember. Since the moment in the forest outside York when her parents had been ambushed and killed!

Consciousness was lost under pressure. Ripping. Screams rent from the very depth of fear. And silence.

'What the hell is wrong with ye now?' A deep voice shattered memory, blue eyes narrowing against the last slant of sun as he caught her wrist and pulled her up from the ground. Close.

She slapped him as he relaxed his grip, all the pent-up

months of worry behind the movement. And when the edge
of Malcolm Kerr's ring caught at his skin, red spilt down
the hard line of his cheek.

He released her immediately and stepped away, the muscles
along his jaw rippling as he lifted his hand to the wound.

'Mother of Mary, are ye a crazy woman? Has David
joined me to a cackle-head?'

She made herself be still, placing her fingers across the
beating terror in her heart and waited for retribution.

None came.

No true sharp blade into the soft folds of her throat, no
well-aimed kick or clenched fist. Nothing except for a
silence that was stark against the shrill, quick call of a
forest bird nesting for the night.

His men melted back, leaving them alone. Grace could
just make out their forms through the leaves of the trees
thick in the glade.

'Do ye have a death wish?'

'No.' She whispered the word. Mouthed it. No time to
even think of stammering, for the light in his eyes held her
transfixed. No empty threat here. No quiet warning.

'Give me your right hand.'

She hid it behind her back, away from him. What did he
want her hand for? To cut it off at the wrist? To break her
fingers one by one by one? To slash his initial into the lines
of her palm?

'Give me your hand, Grace.'

She hated the way her chin began to wobble, hated the
tears that welled in her eyes and the aching fear in her

throat. Hated the way too that her arm came forwards. Towards him.

He took her middle finger, gently, and removed the ring. She felt the roughened skin of his palm and saw the marks of scars under a cloth he wore around his wrist before he let her go.

No, not scars. A brand. A circle dissected by two lines. Indigo. Complex.

'This ring is a family heirloom. My grandmother holds the other half of a matching pair and I am certain that she would wish it back.' For a second he held it before depositing it in his sporran. Gone from her.

Memory!

She began to shake, badly, her teeth chattering together even as she tried to stop them, and, without meaning to, she closed her fingers over the place where the ring had been and buried her hand in the copious folds of her gown.

Relief and the release of a duty and a lie! She thanked him silently for the taking of it.

Lachlan caught his breath and cursed this ridiculous farce that the King had burdened him with. More than twenty years of selfless service repaid by the fetter of marriage to a woman who was scared of her own shadow. If it wasn't so permanent, he might have laughed. Indeed, he had seen the puzzled faces of his men as they tried to fathom out the character of his new wife, and failed. The whispered asides told him that they appreciated her about as little as did the echoes of laughter.

She had hit him!

His frightened mouse of a wife had hit him. Hard. And in the shadowed depths of her amber eyes he had recognised what he so often saw in his own.

Secrets.

Taking a breath, he tried to lighten his voice.

'We still have a few hours of travelling yet as I mean to cross the border north of Carlisle.'

'We c-c-c-cannot m-m-make y-y-your k-k-k-keep?' Lord, her stammer was worsening by the moment. He wondered if she would be able to string even two words together by the time they had reached his castle.

'Nay, it will be safer to camp in the Borders.'

Stressing the word 'safer', he saw the calculations of a walked distance clouding her focus.

'Lord, help me,' he muttered and wished that he was at home in the arms of his mistress.

But he wasn't. He was stuck with a woman who stuttered and shook and lied, and was scared of horses.

Lady Grace Stanton. Nay, he amended as he mounted and pulled her up in front of him, Lady Grace Kerr, now.

His wife.

He made mental calculations as to how many hours he would ever truly be required to spend in her company and was heartened to determine that it would be very few. Perhaps he was more like his father than he had thought, and the realisation made him uneasy.

Freezing. She was freezing. Even with a cloak and blanket and three shawls laid across her she could not stop the shaking that had woken her up a good hour ago. And now she needed to relieve herself. Desperately.

It was dark. Black. The forest trees stretched towards an inky sky, and the moon, that had been high when they had finally reached this place, had fallen, a small and weak slice of crescent on the horizon, surrounded by mist.

Ten feet away Lachlan Kerr lay on the dirt without a scrap of blanket or pillow, the dim light from the fire showing the beaded drops of dew threaded through his night-black hair. Even asleep he held his dirk across his thigh, fingers curled around the shaft in habit.

Standing, she began to move across to him, meaning to shake him awake, but his eyes were open at the first whisper of sound and he was up on his haunches in a quick and easy grace.

'I need to relieve myself.'

He did not budge, question easily seen on his brow.

'It's v-very dark,' she continued and looked towards the trees on the edge of the clearing.

Amazement began to etch out a heavy line on his brow. 'Ye want me to take you?'

'Not to w-w-watch, y-y-you understand. Just to k-k-keep watch.' Damn. Her stutter was back badly and she pressed at the soft skin at the base of her neck to try to ease the tightness.

'Keep watch against what?' His laughter was hard.

The ghosts of the dead and the souls of the nearly living, pressed close against the thin veneer of time.

'I am n-n-not sure.' Uncertainty leached the movement

from her limbs. Should she chance it? Could she walk into the dark, dark forest under a nothing moon and be safe?

Ginny's screams and then silence. Stephen's whispers to make it right. Below them a deep chasm and above them a blue, blue sky.

'Grace?' Lachlan Kerr's voice was close and she saw that he had moved up beside her, no longer laughing.

'Come. I'll take ye.' His fingers were warm against her skin, even through the cloth at her elbow, and she was pleased for the support as they walked across the uneven ground towards the river.

When they reached a glade that offered a little privacy, he stopped and disengaged her arm. 'I will wait here.'

'You promise. You w-w-won't go back? You w-w-won't leave me here…?'

She hoped that he could not see the mounting flush on her skin.

'If we dinna come back soon, my men will investigate.' This time something akin to amusement laced his words.

Lord. And she had lost time already with her chatter. Stepping away from him, she crept behind a tree, keeping the shape of the Laird in her vision. When she was finished, she rejoined him and looked up into the sky.

'Do you e-e-ever wonder if there is anything out th-th-there? Any other place like this one, I mean?'

'No.'

His reply was short, but it did not deter her.

'My father once t-told me of the ideas of Aristarchus of Samos. He wrote that the Earth r-revolved around the Sun.'

'And you believed it?'

'I do, though I can hear in your t-tone you do not.'

'The holy scriptures would say that the Earth is the centre of everything.' He frowned as he looked up. 'A useful ploy to further their own cause, I should imagine.'

'Their cause? You sp-speak like a disbeliever?'

'Once I was not,' he returned obliquely. 'Your stammer seems remarkably lessened tonight.'

'Oh, it only is b-b-bad when I th-th-think about it.'

She tripped on the root of a tree and his hand shot out to balance her body against his.

And for a moment, with the heavens around them and the silence of the very early morning, Grace felt a sense of safety that she had not felt in a long, long time.

Her wedding night. It was not as dreadful as she might have otherwise expected. A husband who had accompanied her into the trees and stayed when she had asked him to. A man who had listened to her explanation of the stars above them with at least a pretended interest and whose arm had steadied her against falling. She tried to still the shivering that had overtaken her and was glad when they reached the clearing.

'We will be breaking camp in about two hours and as it is a long ride home I would advise ye to get some sleep.'

'If w-we were to w-walk, how long would it take?'

Laughter was his only response as he settled himself down, fire highlighting his face.

'Go to sleep, Grace,' he muttered and closed his eyes.

She liked the way he said her name, his accent giving the plain shortness of it a hint of the exotic. Snuggling into her blankets, she felt for her wedding ring. It was an emerald set in yellow gold and engraved on the inside with his initials. L.K. She had seen it in the earlier light.

From this small distance his profile was distinct. The most handsome Laird in all of Scotland. She had heard that said of him each time some soul had uttered his name, which was ironic given her own lack of any charm, though she supposed that a sizeable dowry had its way of talking. Her fingers pressed the numbed welts on her thighs and she felt the hollow ache of all that she was.

Ugly. Beneath her clothes as well. She accepted the summation of her appearance now without question, and made it her habit to seldom look into any mirror. Biting down on tears, she hated the aching lump in her throat. She was tired of wishing herself otherwise, tired of the groundless hope of some miraculous cure for the dry skin she was afflicted with, and the stutter. Taking a deep breath, she willed composure and shut her eyes.

She sat on the royal dais, watching her husband in a joust, her scarf upon his sleeve as he declared himself her champion, her knight, before thundering towards his opponent. And when it was finished and he had easily won, he knelt before her in an act of homage, the ritual of courtly love causing the faces of the other ladies about them to wish it was their favour he donned, their love that he sought...

In her sleep she smiled.

* * *

Lachlan listened as she rearranged her blankets, amazed at the fact that she should need so many layers against a night he felt was almost…warm.

One foot was visible from where he sat, its smallness swamped by a thick woollen stocking. Grace Stanton was nothing like the tales he had heard of her at court. She was unusual, to be sure, but there was something about her that intrigued him. Her imagination, he decided after further thought, as he remembered the softness of her skin when he had steadied her arm to make certain that she did not fall.

She wanted to walk to Belridden and she believed that the stars circled the sun according to an ancient Greek astronomer. He thought of the manuscripts explaining the heavens his father had brought home from Anjou and wondered where they were now. Sold like the rest of the Kerr treasures, he suspected, a further sop to an escalating gambling habit.

Lachlan had barely thought of his father for years and yet here in the space of a day he had thought about him twice. Good times. Before the drink had made Hugh crazy and soft regret had spiralled into sheer and brutal hatred.

Nothing lasted for ever. Not laughter. Not happiness. And certainly not love. The only thing you could count on was the land, and the Kerr land was in sore need of the attention that the Stanton gold would give it.

That was all he expected. Anything else would lead to the disappointment that he was far more familiar with.

He laid his head down against the dirt.

Ever since his return to Scotland it had been a struggle. Government had almost ceased to exist under Robert the High Steward and it had been hard to reassert the authority of his king against the vested interests of landowners made powerful from the long years without covenant. Lord, if David did not step up to rule them, they would rule him, and the murder of the royal mistress was testimony to that.

Lachlan pulled his hair free and shook the length in the night air. Under the Bruce all this might have been so much easier, and for the thousandth time he wished that Robert Keith, the trainer of arms in Normandy, had insisted on a more rigorous tutorship for David.

Everything was uncertain and dangerous with the rebellion of powerful men afoot and yet here he was, dragging a wife home to a land he barely knew. A wife who now lay on her side with her hands clasped beneath her face and the wild redness of her hair a long curtain on the ground beside her.

She was not as plain as he had been told. He wished suddenly that she might open those eyes that were so direct and begin to talk again to him. It had, after all, been a long time since a woman in his company had not reverted to the wiles of flirtation and coquetry, and the change was refreshing. The red stocking she wore on her right foot had also come astray with her disturbed slumber and her ankles were more than shapely.

Lord, he thought to himself, and he turned over to find sleep, trying not to listen to the soft and muffled breathing of his unusual new wife.

Chapter Three

Connor crouched down beside him in the morning before the dawn had properly settled, smouldering anger on his face.

'Your wife had this with her.' He dropped a small jewelled box on the dirt beside him; Lachlan knew the casing immediately.

'How did you find it?'

'It fell out of a layer of clothes as we transferred the contents from her chest into our saddlebags. Ian's horse was suffering under the weight of the thing, you see, and we thought to distribute it around.'

'Does she know ye took it?'

'She dinna see if that's what you are asking.'

Lachlan nodded and jammed the thing in his sporran, making certain it was hidden.

Malcolm had been given the heirloom on his thirteenth birthday by their grandfather, and when the precious stones on the lid had winked against the new light of morning, the bare memory of his brother caught Lachlan anew with the way it had all ended.

'Who else knows?' He took a quick glance at the form of his still-sleeping wife.

'Ian saw it. And James. Do ye think Malcolm gave it to her?'

'Knowing the worth of the thing, I doubt it, but say nothing to anyone else, and seek the silence of Ian and James.' His words trailed off, something disturbing him in the presence of a treasure Malcolm had held such fondness for.

'You would protect her?'

'For now.'

'If Eleanor finds out she had it…'

'She won't.'

'Your grandmama is a wily woman, Lach, and she has always believed that your brother was murdered. Perhaps it was your wife who killed him?'

Lach shook his head. 'If Grace Stanton killed Malcolm, it will be me who deals with her. Understand?'

But Connor was not finished. 'Our king could not expect you to stay married to a murderer.'

'The king wants these lands strong and with her dowry the lives of all those at Belridden will be safer.'

'And you? What of your life? What of the nights you lie asleep in your marriage bed with the full bare skin of your throat exposed?'

'You think she will be there beside me?'

Smothering fury, he looked over at Grace clambering from her pile of blankets. The dress she wore was stained and creased and yet as she stretched into wakefulness the sun behind caught her hair, long and fire red, molten silk unfurling down her back to reach along the rounded lines of her hips. She tempted him and left him feeling unreasonably irritated.

'Tell the Lady of Kerr that we will be breaking camp in half an hour. Find her someone to ride with.'

'You won't be taking her with you?'

'I won't.'

'She can ride with me, then.'

'Very well.' Lachlan tossed his plaid over his shoulder and completely ignored his wife's worried frown.

Turning to the forest, he walked just outside the lines of saplings towards the river, taking a moment to contemplate all that had happened in the last few days.

His life had been turned upside down, yet some things stayed exactly the same, and the betrayal that had dogged his years from boyhood was as repellent in this wife as it had been in the last one.

A gap in the trees allowed him another glimpse of the new Lady of Kerr as she tried to wipe the marks of dust from her costly gown, the fine wool of her skirt drawn tight across the generous outline of her bottom.

Heat rushed into his loins and he felt an odd unbalance as the forest and his men melted away into nothingness. Lord, what was happening? Had she placed some tonic in the wine at Grantley, some potion to mask his reasoning and raise his lust? His mistress was full-blooded and well endowed, the wares on show offered without condition, but he had not felt this…excitement with her.

Not once.

Grace Stanton with her fire-red hair and welt-roughened

skin should have run a poor second to Rebecca's charms and yet…dressed in a high-necked gown with little showing save the top of her hands and the curve of her throat she was…sensual. The thought amazed him.

How?

How did she do that?

How did a woman with so little in the way of obvious endowments manage to be alluring? Had his brother felt it too?

He refused to follow further down that particular track, though he was niggled by the question of whether the Kerrs were to be for ever cursed by the words of Alec Dalbeth.

'Your keep shall be a ruin and any love that you foster will be as dust in the darkening days of your clan.'

It had been years since his father had banished the priest from their lands, one arm around the mistress that had caused the chasm and the other on a bottle. Clutching. Tight. But the words shouted back into the space between the departing horses and the front portal of Belridden had stuck. Darkness had come in the form of strong drink, and his father, on seeing the sins of his ways too late, had taken the easy path out.

It was Malcolm and he who had found him dangling from the middle beam of the chapel roof, a half-finished tankard smashed beneath his feet, as if he had taken one last sip to see him through the gates of Hell.

He cursed, hating the weakness of a man whom he had once admired, when a noise to one side of the stream slowed his movements. Bending down, he scoured the far-off bank. A group of men were creeping through the under-growth, metal glinting from the first rays of the sun. The Elliots or the Johnstones, neighbouring clans whom the Kerrs had no reason to trust. From this distance he could not quite make out the muted colours worn.

Three minutes, he guessed, till they rounded the slower part of the river and crossed. Unsheathing his claymore, he backtracked with care. Twenty against forty. The odds were good if it came to a head and he'd be hard pressed to find a better group of soldiers around him.

Would that be enough? He refused to think about it not being so even as he began to run, a branch swiping hard against his face and another slashing his shins.

Grace was standing against the bough of a tree to one side of the camp as he fled through the last saplings and she turned towards him as the others did, eyes bright with fear. He knew she was trying to say something, but could not quite get the words out. Dragging her against him, he placed her in the middle of the circle his men were forming.

'Shield your head and shut your eyes,' he shouted at her as he took his own place between Con and Ian, the outlines of the other group now visible between the thinning forest. More than forty. Lach's grip tightened on his sword and he made himself breathe.

Grace watched Lachlan Kerr's back and saw the way he brought in breath. Once, twice, three times and then stillness, the echo of a malevolent danger harnessed with a steely control.

Magnificent. The thought burst from nowhere as he

raised his sword, the strength of his knotted muscles rippling free. Waiting. Wanting. A man tempered in war and killing and fear. She could see the lines where blades had cut against the solid muscle of his forearm when the fabric in his shirt fell back, white against the brownness of his skin, tense, honed. All the forest still as the party from across the river gained the clearing.

'Who goes there?' Her husband's words held no inflection of fear. She felt calmed by his very equanimity.

A big man facing them stepped forwards. 'Alistair Elliot. And I dinna remember giving ye invite to cross my lands, Kerr.'

'You had no word from David?'

'The King?' Uncertainty shallowed out the other's voice and the glances of the men behind sharpened.

'I have it on David's authority to collect my wife from her home in England.'

Grace knew in the hollow lack of humour the truth that such an admission must have cost him.

A wife who looked like her and English, and a battle that could easily cost the lives of some of his soldiers.

The man opposite shook his head, catching sight of her at the exact same moment that he did so, arrant disbelief in his eyes. The tensing of the muscles in Lachlan Kerr's jaw was worrying as all around her the men closed ranks, drawing in on the spaces between them, a solid wall of protection for a woman that they could feel no allegiance to, no favour for. The thought stunned her. They would fight and die to keep her safe just because Kerr willed it.

'Your wife looks as though she may be ailing. Are ye sure it's the right woman ye have picked?' The offence was measured and Grace tensed, the heavy mantle of insolence falling between them, a breathing living thing that smote good sense and reason.

Lachlan gestured his men back and the space in the clearing widened. 'Ye'd be willing to sacrifice your men for the slur you have just offered or are you man enough to stand and fight me alone?' His glance was pale-blue-cold and for the first time the other man stepped back, hand running to the sword at his side, testing the grip. Waiting.

Time quivered and the whispers of those who began to question snaked over silence.

'I'd give my word that if you were to fight me and win, every blade we harbour would be yours to keep.' Lachlan Kerr's voice held the bland edge of indifference, as if his death was but a trifling consideration and the cache of armoury a greater prize.

'And I could take your word on it?'

'My word, or your men's lives, it worries me not. Or are ye afraid?'

When the newcomer pulled up his sword and slashed suddenly, shiny slick steel missed Lachlan Kerr's throat by a matter of mere inches and Grace had to rise on tiptoes to see over the shoulder of the man in front, her heart beating so hard that she was certain that the sound of it must be heard.

If Lachlan Kerr was killed, what then?

Would she be taken back to Grantley or would someone else here claim her? She doubted the men from Belridden would want to let go of her money so easily and doubted too the fineness of their morals. Lord, the man who even now circled his adversary, waiting for a chance to strike, was becoming her protector, even given his lack of caring.

The hollow sound of steel against steel rang so loud that she found herself placing her hands across her ears just to dim the noise. Not pretty. Not easy. No dainty practised fight this one, but the raw lunges of two men who would kill each other should the chance present itself. And it nearly did as Lachlan parried, his feet hitting the roots of an elm behind and tipping him off balance, the wicked sharpness of his opponent's blade making him pay for the mistake in a deep slash down his left arm. The soldiers near her mumbled, and Lachlan bade them back.

'Nay. Be still. It's a scratch and my word has been given.'

He did not look at her as he said it, did not in any way include her in the moment. Grace tried to catch his glance to show him that she was at least grateful for his protection, but he allowed her nothing. His very indifference to his fate angered her, made the whole basis of this marriage even bleaker. She wondered how much longer she would have a husband, so careless was he of his life?

With the settling of the fight a different rhythm seemed to come, a closer, finer combat, thrust and counter-thrust, the sweat building on both men's brows belying the chill in this part of Scotland in early August. Lachlan Kerr moved with a grace seldom seen in a big man, his every movement carefully honed and delivered, nothing left to chance as he came in again and again against his opponent's weakening thrusts. And then the other man was down on the ground, a sharp swordpoint pinning him motionless and pressing deep. Horror overcame disbelief. Her husband would kill a defenceless man and risk the wrath of God and the eternal promise of an afterlife?

'No!' The desperate shout distracted everyone and all eyes came upon her. Without conscious thought she drew herself up to her tallest form and made herself speak. 'H-H-He h-h-holds no weapon and if you sh-sh-sh-should kill him, God w-w-will punish y-y-your soul.'

Silence met the statement and then the budding of anger. From everyone.

'Is she a gomeral or just plain saft in the heid?'

The dark-haired man spoke from his position on the ground, the words strangling with such caustic incredulity that pure wrath replaced Grace's softer anger and she made no effort to harness it. 'You m-m-might c-c-c-consider the message of m-m-my words r-r-rather than the s-s-stutter in them, sir.'

'*A Dhia, thoir cobhair*, she insults me again?'

Lachlan unexpectedly began to smile as he released the throat of his foe, allowing the man to roll over.

'Get up, Elliott, and be thankful that my wife has not yet worked out the ways of the Scots. She thinks her truth does you a service.'

A quivering waiting filled the air around them, sifting out options as to a way forwards.

'Then if I hear you have smothered her in the night, Kerr, I will know the reason why.'

He laughed and anger dissipated, and as the group from the river collected their armour and withdrew, Grace was finally allowed from the prison of her tight band of men.

'They d-d-did not l-l-leave their w-weapons and you w-w-won.'

'Ye think that? Ye think that I won?'

For a second Grace imagined Lachlan Kerr would raise his hand against her, so forcibly did she feel the fire of his fury.

'Next time when you think to order me, wife, know that you will be punished. Severely.'

He swiped at the wound on his arm as he pushed past her, the fresh red flow of blood marking the trail of his passage into the trees.

Horrified, she glanced at the ground, not wanting to meet any other censure. Connor was the first to speak.

'You can ride home with me.' When he turned away before she could argue, she felt tears prick behind her tired eyes. No one fostered manners here. No one held to the polite tones of normal deportment. She had saved a life and a soul and these men were too arrogant to realise the help she had given them. With her head held high, she leaned against the bough of an oak and contemplated just how far in walking distance it was to the Kerr's keep of Belridden.

Lachlan could barely stop the roiling anger from bubbling over into a shout of wrath. His wife had shamed him and he knew with a certainty that the news would be travelling around the Marches like wildfire come the evening. The Laird of Kerr brought to task by the plain Englishwoman he had been forced to marry.

Damn it. He had told her to shut her eyes and hide her head and instead…instead she had spoken with her quavery voice, stuttering a truth in the way that only she could have imagined it. His hands tightened around his aching arm and he looked down at the injury, the sides of skin peeling away and leaving the wound wide open.

He should have killed Elliot, for if this cut should fester then he himself would be the man marked for the hereafter.

A wavering sadness counteracted fury. His first wife had been a harlot and this one was a blabbering loudmouth. Dalbeth's curse weighed on his shoulders, and the banal and aimless void of living stretched long and lonely into a future he could no longer imagine or care about.

He drew in breath and listened to the birds in the trees. Life. His life. This one and only life. He was no longer a religious man, though he hid his lack of belief well, stacked against the certainty of the Kerrs' bad luck and the vagaries of a more primitive faith. He had lived by the sword for so long now he could barely remember what it had been like before.

Once he had been young, hopeful, running through the forests to the north with his brother, and seeing in the shape of leaves or the colour of the first flowers of spring, a God-given beauty, a plan, a way of living that did not incorporate so much death and loss and despair.

'If you kill him, God will punish you.' Grace's words, give or take the stutter. She was a woman who still believed in the power of a soul and in the very darkness that his should

be cast into. He grimaced. She knew nothing of his life and could not understand that it was well past time to worry about his particular salvation or to chart the celestial journey of any humanity that still lingered inside him.

His life! He remembered his fingers around the neck of those who would support David's enemies when the talking had come to nothing and the splintered and isolated monarchy was again threatened. God, he wiped the hair from his eyes and said a prayer, not believing in the message but comforted by the habit of it.

Nay, the bleating goodness of a woman of principle was not for the likes of him, buried as he was in the netherworld of survival.

David had no notion of what he destroyed under the auspices of politics. Her life for one: Grace Stanton-Kerr and her bloody stuttered truths. Running his fingers through the length of his hair, he wondered again about the validity of what was whispered by royal enemies who would sacrifice the monarchy. Yet the alternative bore down on him like a heavy harbinger of doom. No king? The mantle of tradition was preferable to the absence of it.

Anarchy!

He had seen it in the eyes of the powerful magnates and the sons of Balliol, and heard it in the words of Edward of England's detractors and Philip the Sixth's enemies.

Change for the better? This was a risky hope pinned on rebellion and paid for in the blood of men. Countrymen!

Finding at last what he sought he stripped the sphagnum moss and mulched it between his fingers, spitting on the pink mass to form a paste before smearing it across his wound. The astringent flared and he swore softly, but held the potion in place until the pain ceased altogether. His mother had taught him about the medicines found in the forest.

His mother!

When she had died in childbirth, the light had gone out of Belridden, and had been out ever since.

As he pulled down the sleeve of his jacket, the angry sound of his new spouse's voice broke across his thoughts.

'I w-w-w-will not get up on that h-h-horse.'

Con's reply was surprisingly patient.

'It is a long way to the keep, my Lady, and it is in my mind that your brogans are hardly up to the task.'

'B-brogans?'

'Shoes, my Lady.'

'F-f-fetch me my h-h-husband.'

Even at this distance Lachlan could hear the aristocratic edge to her command and knew too that Con would be no match at all for her. With resolve he strode forwards, breaking from the shelter of the forest to find a ring of men regarding his wife.

'She will ride. With me.'

The fight he could see in her eyes came quickly to the surface and Connor moved back, relieved of his need to argue further.

'I c-c-cannot.'

In answer he simply strode forwards and threw her across his shoulders, her shapely backside brushing the side of his cheek. Her fingers scratched at his back and he was pleased for the thick covering of his plaid and highland shirt. 'Put me down you…you…blackguard,' she finally said, the semi-curse a long way from the language that he was much more used to. 'Put me down this very moment or I shall…'

'What?' he countered as he dumped her on his horse, keeping her balanced there with a sheer dint of will as he swung up behind her. His arm hurt like hell from the tussle. 'What exactly will you do?'

She was silent and he refrained from mentioning how much better her stutter was, though with his thighs pressing on hers and her back warm against his stomach Lachlan was more than aware of his damnably traitorous body rising to attention with each passing second. The scent of her filled his nostrils, the scent of woman and heat, long strands of her hair burnishing his skin with fire-flame red.

Her heart drummed at thrice the pace of his, racing in the slender curve of her throat and as her fingers tightened over his legs she began to shake.

'Zeus is a fine mount. He obeys my commands unquestionably. You have nothing to fear.'

Sitting on his horse in the clearing with his men busying themselves for departure, Lachlan could feel in the silence every ear upon them.

She did not answer, but he felt her feet fold up as if she would be completely free of any stirrup that hung there and heard the quietly whispered prayers. Over and over again.

Shifting in his seat, he tried to summon back anger, but the zealous ardency of her invocations amused him and her skin, exposed at the nape of her neck, made him catch his breath.

Nothing about this woman added up and her shivers of fright made him wonder. Had she been unnerved somehow by a horse? There was so much about her that he did not know. When she had lifted her skirts yesterday no mark of an accident had been visible, and yet she limped!

Lord! Putting all thought aside, he concentrated on the narrowing path in front of them, loose rocks falling into the nothingness of the gully below as the mounts picked their way through.

'Y-your horse is v-v-very obedient.' The whisper was soft.

'Unlike my wife,' he returned, regretting it when she stiffened and did not speak again.

They stopped by a river three hours from home to rest the horses. When he slipped from the saddle, he was surprised that she made no effort to follow him, given her preference for walking, although the reason for her reticence was obvious a moment later.

She could barely stand when he helped her down. Placing her hand around his, she clung on, the leg with the limp buckling under the weight of her body.

Turning a brighter shade of red than even her hair, Lachlan was aware of the effort the ride must have cost as she tried to stand unaided, the shaking sending her teeth to chattering.

'H-how far n-now?'

'Belridden lies about an hour from here.' He found himself minimising the distance even though he meant not to. Damn it. Everything about her irritated him and yet here he was halving the journey home in an effort to lessen the worry in her eyes and the weary cadence he could hear in her voice.

He watched her nod and watched too as she hobbled a little way from him, awkwardly placing her weight as she went.

If she fell… He made himself stop and turn away.

God, Grace Stanton had been with them for all of thirty hours, in which she had shamed him in front of an enemy and split his cheek open with his dead brother's ring. She had a stutter that hurt his ears to listen to, and a fear of life that boded badly for the wilder climes of his own estate, and that was without taking into account her damaged leg and a skin condition that looked at best more than a little itchy.

Yet despite everything Lachlan found himself smiling, for there was something about her that was…brave. A woman who was her own person. A lady of means who believed in the power of God and stood up for his soul with the crystal-clear goodness of one who had never been confronted with the bad.

Pureness was a potent power in the face of suspicion and doubt, he suddenly decided, and a quality that Belridden had long been bereft of.

He imagined taking her to his bed, undressing her, feeling the tightness of her sex around him. He could take her tonight when they arrived at Belridden.

The throb in his loins settled hard against his shirt and he adjusted the fullness as he walked. Would she be virgin or would his brother have known her intimately? He hoped not. He had never had a virgin before, preferring the ease of well-experienced women. Yet he saw suddenly the appeal of such an encounter. Everything to her would be new. And in the unknown he sensed an aphrodisiac that he had not before pondered upon.

Connor interrupted his thoughts as he walked. The sound of his wife's prayers droned on through the air.

'Lady Grace is very devout…'

'She'll need to be to survive Belridden.'

Irritation rose to a newer level at the continued and fervent incantations and when Grace Stanton finally came up behind him he did not even try to hide his displeasure.

'I came to a-a-apologise,' she stated quietly. 'A-a-and to say that I was j-j-just trying to h-help you.'

'Help me?' Her small smile of agreement incensed him further. 'Help me?' he added again as he watched her nod, incredulity replacing wrath. Did she have no idea at all as to the consequences of her behaviour? Another darker thought skimmed across the first one. Was she bating him?

His arm throbbed. His keep was still far off and beside him stood a woman who had neither the intellect nor the inclination to understand his anger. When his fingers shot out to lace around her wrist, he could not find it in him to lessen the bleakness of his tone.

'You are my wife by the edict of David, King of the Scots. Do nothing more to annoy me. Do you understand that?'

He felt certain that the fright in her eyes would allow her to think about the precariousness of her situation and to mould her behaviour into an appropriate response.

'No, I do not q-q-quite.'

Amazement at her effrontery left him speechless.

'It is my d-d-duty as your w-wife to p-p-protect you, too.'

His bitter laughter was loud as he removed his hand. 'You are here to provide Belridden with an heir, nothing else. And protection is my domain. I do not require any such thing from you.'

As she turned away, he saw that her hand no longer threaded through the ornate rosary beads.

Chapter Four

Her husband of two days was looking across at a woman standing to one side of the room. A woman with flaxen hair, her blue eyes meeting his in a complicity that even at this distance was unmistakeable. For just a moment Grace felt a quick thud of envy, but she pressed it down. For her to presume love from a man like the Laird of Kerr was foolish and completely unreasonable.

He had a mistress, a beautiful mistress, and when he walked across and kissed her soundly in front of everyone in the Great Hall, Grace knew exactly her position here.

She was a breeding wife, the provider of money and an heir. Not a lover or a friend, but a woman to beget progeny. Lawful progeny. Boys who would some day take on the mantle of this place and make it stronger. War and fighting and reiving were the life-blood of the Borderland keeps after all, and she swallowed back singular disappointment.

Belridden mirrored the sudden coldness she felt inside, showing no glimmer of any redeeming feature in the draughty and ill-kempt hall. The wind whistled in through wooden shutters and the rough sleeping mat-tresses littering the floor had not been cleared away. Half-eaten food scraps and mangy dogs lay beneath a high table that had neither linen on it nor tapestries behind it. Impoverished and meagre, Belridden stood like a sentinel on the very last edge of civilisation. The rolling green pastures of Grantley, the manor house with its garde-robes and its luxury and an ease of both language and weather seemed so far away in this unfamiliar and uneasy landscape.

She shook her head, seeing in that moment how appeal-ing her dowry must have been to a laird struggling with day-to-day expenses. Nothing here looked as if it had been attended to for decades. Even the occupants inside the keep looked ragged, their simple tunics and shifts dotted with repairs. She saw in their covert glances just exactly what they thought of her. Nobody smiled. Nobody welcomed her. Nobody hid the knowledge of her place here or sheltered her from the fondling of the Laird and his mistress, the woman's arms now full along the rise of Lachlan Kerr's buttocks.

She had been fooling herself on the journey north that this alliance could be anything more than a simple union of need—his need of legitimate heirs and her need of a husband. Any sort of husband given her advanced years. Even the brother of a man she had loathed.

Taking in a breath, she swallowed back panic. Lachlan Kerr's ring on her finger denoted ownership in a circle of promise and submission and any ill-timed rebellion now could ruin things completely. In children she might find great happiness, and surely in the sharing and shaping of young lives some common ground could be formed.

His hand at her elbow surprised her.

'If you follow me, I'll show ye where you're to sleep.' The woman he had fondled watched from the other side of the room, warning in her eyes as their glances met. With dignity Grace smiled, hoping to give the impression of an airy unconcern even as she hid her shaking fingers in the generous train of her woollen dress.

Lachlan Kerr signalled his men to pick up her possessions and turned towards a door she had not noticed before. Lifting her skirts to avoid the hem being stained further, Grace was surprised by the breadth of a tower and by the warmth of a cosy solar off a hallway. A fire burned in a large grate, a coiled rush mat on the ground before it. To one end was a raised cubby with a mattress spread on wooden slats and covered in an intricate green-and-red cloth. A footstool, a table and a sturdy oaken chair completed the furniture.

When the men placed her things on the floor and departed, Lachlan Kerr closed the door behind them.

Alone. A silence widening with possibility. When he reached out and laid his hand across the swell of her bosom, the clench of her teeth worried the soft flesh on the inside of her mouth.

Blood. She tasted it and swallowed, keeping still as his fingers wandered down to the curve of her hips and the line of her bottom. Through the fine cloth of her gown her skin burned and her heartbeat, already quickened, doubled its pace yet again.

When he laughed and moved back, she felt the blaze of embarrassment more forcibly than she ever had before.

'I will take ye tonight after supper. A woman will be sent to see to your needs.'

His voice was deep and she saw in his eyes the unmistakable flare of sex, and the sharp rush of prescience almost made her faint.

Beat, beat, beat.

Blood in her throat and in her stomach and in a place between her legs where there had only ever been stillness.

I will take you tonight. A duty. An insignificant thing. *After supper.*

'I th-th-th-think th-th-that w-w-we sh-should w-w-wait.'

'Wait for what?' he returned with impatience even as he opened up the portal to leave.

For love. For softness. For the blossoming of feeling and hope and promise. She shook her head as the words rushed around in her mind and watched the easy way he left her, his thoughts on other obligations that waited outside.

Standing perfectly still she reached one hand across her breast just as he had, the quick thrill of ardour returning, bold with thoughts of something she did not comprehend. Imagining. Skin against skin. Her eyes flew open and all the pleasurable feeling exited in one single rush. Her hand went to her damaged leg, the knots of red-welted scars overlaid with pearl. She was a flawed wife.

Peg-leg. Ugly. Red-head. She scratched at the creases of skin at her elbows as she contemplated options. The children at Grantley had been told to be kind as she was growing up, though many a boy had not heeded the special advice given about how to handle the withdrawn and newly orphaned thirteen-year-old Grace. Their taunts still pierced her equanimity sometimes, a reminder of reality when her mind took her on other journeys of wishful thinking.

Would she be able to stay in her clothes for this *'taking'*? Could the expanse of skin between her ankle and her knee be enough for a man like Lachlan Kerr to dwell on before he laid his seed on her stomach? Grace frowned and wondered where this seed would go next. Without a mother, and as the oldest of the female cousins, she had had no one to ask about the proprieties of marriage and its expectations. Of course she knew children were a product of this thing that a married couple did after marriage, but the mechanics of a swollen belly as a result of 'the act' eluded her. She had tried to ask Stephen of it once, but he had not answered, avoiding her company until he left again for London. So she had desisted from further questions, reasoning that, as an ageing and plain woman, she might never need to know the answer anyway.

Until today. Until the hours that led to supper, suspense vied with dread in a very even measure.

Lachlan cut into his rondel dagger with the flat side of a water stone, angling the blade so that the full bite of it was in contact, and rubbing till a burr began to form. Testing the sharpness to see if the edge grabbed, he cursed as the honed blade slid into the soft base of his right thumb.

He swore roundly, before placing down both stone and

blade and wiping blood against the linen of his long shirt. He felt keyed up, nervous almost, the fear he had seen in his wife's eyes somehow…important.

Could this be her first time? At twenty-six! Lord, the whole idea unnerved him. He had been less than half her age when the fifteen-year-old daughter of a French knight had asked him into the deserted tack room of her father's stables and showed him exactly what it was he had been missing. When their illicit affair had been discovered, he'd been hauled off to the battlefield of Vironfosse in Vervins with Philip the Sixth, his back tanned with the sharp end of a whip and the sure-fire knowledge that he would never bed an unmarried girl again. And he hadn't.

He frowned. He would bed Grace Stanton and hope that issue would be forthcoming quickly.

The ghosts of the past quietened under his plans and, digging into his sporran, he found his brother's ring and turned the rubies into the light. Remembering.

Ruth. His first wife! He had taken this very ring from her finger as she had been buried in the consecrated ground beside the chapel because he had not uttered a word.

Not one.

And the secrets that simmered beneath the liturgy of honour and esteem and integrity spoken at her burial had remained untold because of the baby, her skin marked close with blue veins. The bastard progeny of his brother and stillborn, as if God in all his omnipotence had smote her breathless.

Hannah. He had called her that after his mother, because

she had needed at least a name. Grinding his teeth together, he stood. Time should have leached some of the pain but it had not, and when Malcolm had been killed his violently uttered oaths had brought him Grace Stanton.

God, what irony was there in that, he asked himself and went to stand at the window, pulling back a sheath of leather and staring out. The sun was low, falling behind the Cheviots on its journey west. Night time. Almost. The thought of his new wife readying herself for him was surprisingly arousing. Erotic, even. He had instructed his housekeeper to make certain that she bathed, a custom he had adopted daily since his first sojourn into Acquitaine. He hoped that she would not be adorned with too heavy a nightdress. He hoped that her hair would be down. But most of all he hoped that she would not share the trait of Ruth, her sullen inertness at the whole process of lovemaking a decided inhibitor to any enjoyment.

The sun fell now into the darkening dusk, turning the surrounding countryside into hidden shadow. Taking breath, he released it carefully. He felt suddenly like a young boy, the pull of lust strong in his blood.

How would he take Grace? Quick and hard or slow and soft? Up to him. Completely. The flesh between his legs swelled as an unwanted power, all the old betrayals surfacing. He did not want a wife to worry about. He did not want a spouse to watch over to determine if her conscience was clear or not. He did not want the fetter of trust laced again around him, its tethers pulling tighter and tighter with the passing of time.

If she hated him, all this would be so much easier. He

would have her as a wife in name only, to ripen with his children and hold her own counsel. Already he could see how those in his castle had turned against her and he had made no move to make it different. Nay, Grace Stanton with her fire-red hair and her stutter would bear his children and ensure his lineage. That was all.

'*Sheas,*' he muttered into the silence. At thirty-three he was too damn old for all this nonsense. Too old to try to mend what was broken, and lust was such a fleeting companion.

Chapter Five

Grace sat on the chair beside her bed and waited. She had dismissed the woman sent to help her dress a good half an hour earlier. The offered bath had been a wonderful surprise and she felt cleaner than she had in days, despite redressing in her sturdy day gown.

When would Lachlan Kerr come demanding her wifely obligations? She guessed it to be some time after the hour of ten and wished that she had the bravery to blow out the row of candles on the table and bar the door, the slats on this side well hewn and heavy. But if she did that it would only be delaying everything until the morrow and she suddenly wanted what it was that would happen now done, so that she could wake in the morning with at least some knowledge of what she faced…for the rest of her life.

Footfalls outside had her tensing, and, tilting her head, she listened to the sound of voices.

Lachlan Kerr and a woman, her voice honey sweet and pleading. His mistress, perhaps? Grace's ire rose at a trill of something that sounded like laughter. And then silence.

The handle turned slowly once and halted, as if he too might be delaying.

Then he was there, shirt bereft of plaid, and for the first time she saw him without a weapon. His hair was plaited at the side of his face into two long strands and the rest of it was down, the line of it reaching past his shoulders, dark black with a thread of silver at his right temple.

Puzzlement showed briefly on his brow.

'Did the housekeeper nae send a maid, then? To help ye dress, ye ken.' His Scottish accent was thicker tonight and she could smell strong brew, even at this distance.

'I-indeed she d-did. B-but I ch-ch-chose to stay in my d-day gown.'

He frowned. 'Are you knowledgeable about the ways of men?' Such a formal question. 'Did your mother tell you about the happenings in the marriage bed?'

She shook her head and a slither of ire threaded across his brow. 'Clothes are no' needed at all.'

Grace felt the blood run from her face. 'I c-c-could not p-possibly…' She stopped. One look at her scars and he would want no more to do with her.

The soft concern she saw in his eyes surprised her as he left the room, returning less than a minute later with pewter mugs and a jug of ale. Pouring out two generous drinks, he handed her one and bade her sit again on the oaken chair. He took his own seat on the side of her bed, facing her.

'I will nae hurt ye beyond what…will be necessary, you understand.'

She nodded, not certain as to what she was understanding or agreeing to. Hurt or acquiescence?

'But my seed must mix wi' yours to form a bairn.'

'A-a-a b-bairn.' Two words and each one hard to say.

Bringing a mug up to her lips, he waited as she took a large sip. Then waited again, his shirt pulling up carelessly across the untanned insides of his thighs, his legs well muscled with dark whorls of hair.

'Did ye nae sleep wi' my brother?' A different question. Unexpected.

When fear ripped through her she hoped that he would take her shaking as a sign of grief.

'I see. But ye loved him, then?'

Looking up, she watched as he took a drink, the froth of the ale smeared across his top lip until he licked it off. A pure shot of anger appeared in his pale blue eyes when she did not dare to form an answer.

'Then I am sorry both for your loss and for what must happen next.'

The dull throbbing in her stomach became stronger as he reached out and took her hand in his own, holding on when she tried in vain to pull back, his thumb tracing across her palm.

Only that, and a small hint of interest grew. The lines that circled his wrist were unfamiliar and foreign and she felt the hardness of toil and war imbued into the very texture of his skin. Danger had its own exhilaration, Grace decided, as the ale began to warm other more forbidden feelings.

The Laird of Kerr neither looked up nor spoke, but his

breath against her hand came faster, as if in such a tiny thing a man as large and obdurate as him could be affected, as if within her was a power that left him vulnerable. Exposed!

Potency surged and her thumb joined his, a modest caress, the whisper of a promise barely made. And here in this unlikely keep, miles from home and with the wind outside, Grace felt…altered. There was no other word for it. A transformation had been effected by his embrace of her, of who she was, plainness forgotten under the promise of what lay between them. Secret and private. Nobody else's business at all.

She was twenty-six and a woman who had not expected the promise of marriage and children, so, even if their tryst should last just this one night, she would be a fool not to relax and enjoy what a man like Lachlan Kerr could show her, teach her. Imagination, after all, lay a poor second to… this, and there had been many a night when she had lain in her bed and fantasised.

Her breath fluttered strangely in her throat, as if the very air was thinner, and his pale eyes watched her, knowing, one finger on the pulse at her wrist.

'If ye do like this, there is verra much more that I would show you, aye.'

'More?' She hardly recognised the sound of her own voice.

'Much more,' he whispered back, his lips now on the soft skin at the base of her throat and trailing downwards, his fingers pulling at the laces of her bodice, deftly untying them and spreading the material around her shoulders. Opened. The slight cold of the air was welcome, cool against warm, another layer of promise and of risk. His hand slipped between linen and flesh, cupping one breast, the flare of his nostrils evident as he determined fullness.

She should have cried out stop, should have blushed at the sheer temerity of what he did, this stranger, this husband only by the will of kings, but she was held mute by the beauty of his touch and breath and challenge.

This was no paltry man of little consequence, no bow-legged gaunt lover with a face to match his figure. Nay, she, Grace Stanton, was being courted by a man who could have easily come straight from her dreams, from the stories she was so used to weaving, from the myths and legends echoing down from the very first gatherings of time.

The sharper flick of his finger on her nipple made her take in breath, and she tried to quell the rush of hope the action engendered as she hardened proud against his thumb, the small nub of her body's desire tight and close, puckered into want.

When he bent down she gasped and tried to pull away, but he suckled hard and her head fell back of its own accord.

Lord, for this minute, just for this minute, she thought, her hand threading through his hair and bringing him closer, as a mother might a child, or a mistress might a lover.

A lover. Candlelight surrounded them, the scent of woman and man, her hand against his breast, nipple hard against her nail, pinching, the ache of lust and passion and the ancient rhythm of love. Faster.

I...will...love...you...for ever.

'Grace.' Her name. She came back with a start, his hand

over hers, holding her to the task, puzzlement in his eyes. 'For a novice you are well versed in the arts of pleasing a man.'

'I copied you.'

No stutter now. It surprised her, this lack of difficulty in speaking and she began again. 'I th-th-thought if I liked it, then you should too.' Not quite as fluid as the last sentence, but still a lot better than her usual difficulty in his company. Lachlan Kerr's eyes ran across her generous curves. She did nothing to cover the nakedness of her full breasts, her bodice now around her waist, her skin translucent against the light of candles.

She felt wanton, careless, the ties of propriety that had always bound her had fallen away under the pledge of union and when he reached out and gathered her to him she went gladly.

Not soft either, but tough and full of promise, his tongue scorched a trail along her lips before plundering her mouth, searching inside, denying her breath, taking her as his wife, his woman, allowing her no resistance or refusal, open and wider, one hand in her hair as he hauled her close, the other fastening over her breast.

Tight bound. No allowance of rejection. The urgency in her body grew, building into thick hot pushes from a place deep within, the voice of it torn from her lips in a punctuated groan as he held her against his shoulder, her whole body jolting in involuntary surges, the quivers of desire surprising them both.

'God.' His voice, as the liquid heat in her uncoiled and flowed, all around her the light of joy and pleasure. More. Lust no longer hidden, her fingers traced the shape of his cheeks and of his jaw and of the line of his throat. Down. Need burned in the fire of his eyes and the harshness of his breath and the fine true shape of his body as he stripped off his shirt, nothing beneath it but man. The wound from the battle with the Elliots was still bound, white cloth against brownness. She hoped it didn't hurt him, but feared it might as he adjusted her arm so that she did not lean against it.

'My turn now.' He reached for the hem of her skirt, frowning as she stopped him.

'The candles.'

'You'd like them out?'

When she nodded, he lifted her on to the bed before leaning over to extinguish them.

Darkness. Shadow. The shape of him against moonbeams.

She had expected to be shocked by the sight of a man's naked body, but wasn't, his buttocks taut and high and his sex hanging hard as he came in close.

With a will of their own her hands wandered towards him, the smooth stretch of skin pulsating as she reached around, quick and then slow. He jolted away as if he had been burned.

'Who taught you this?'

The veins in his neck were raised against firelight and the gleam in his eyes measured shock.

'No one.'

Even his tone did not alarm her. Nay, lying there with her breasts exposed and her fingers exploring his maleness, she felt a kind of exhilaration, as if all the years of her life had been leading up to this one very moment, as if his body was an instrument she had need to practise on, to tune and play with, the melody floating into her with transparent easiness. She could not let him go, her fingers cradling a heavier softness and then exploring further again to the parts behind. When his muscles clenched she smiled.

'Is this allowed?'

He nodded.

'And this?'

He groaned, beads of sweat full now on his brow, black hair plastered to his temple.

'Ahh, Grace,' he said at length. 'If its revenge you want, then you are surely killing me.'

'Revenge?'

Her fingers stilled.

'This marriage of ours. I had no say in any of it and with Malcolm dead…' He faltered as she twisted tighter. '*Deo gratias*. Enough.' His grip clamped across her wrist and he rolled on top in one easy movement, elbows anchoring her to the bed and his eyes close.

'Now I should know you.' His fingers pushed beneath her skirt and on instinct she began to fight. Instantly he stopped.

'It's a willing woman I want, Grace. If you truly mean for me to cease…'

Caught between desire and fright, she opted for the first and lay still.

Lachlan watched her in the pale light of the moon, watched the fight leave her body and the resolve fill her velvet eyes, watched the way she widened her legs and let

him in, ardour making her groan. She was the most respon-
sive woman he had ever known. Already he felt her fingers
explore the place where his did, meeting in her wet warm
centre as he penetrated further. Up and up and inside, the
barrier of her virginity easily felt.

He knew suddenly the power of her maidenhead and the
responsibility of being her first. Breathing in, he tried to
slow down, tried to bring gentleness across the rush of
passion. And couldn't. Straddling her, he plunged, the
thrust of his sex making her move upwards. He was aware
of the small run of blood and her cries, high pitched, before
his mouth closed down over the sound, his tongue lathing
in the same motion as his hips.

This was the 'little death' the French spoke of, this
blending of beings into oneness, stroke after stroke, higher
and higher and letting go, falling into each other, complete.

He could barely catch his breath as he lay there, barely take
in the notion of what had just happened, the last tender ripple
of pleasure between them. Questioning. Wanting. More.

And amber velvet eyes looking straight into his own. No
tears. No regret. No recrimination. The King's edict and the
need of a bairn. Simple logic. There to breed.

He hardened at the very thought, and sitting, brought her
on to his lap, her skirt hiding movement and concealing
what they both could feel.

'Again,' he whispered and her nails raked the skin across
his back deep, as if her hurt should also be his in the second
taking of her innocence.

Deeper. And the hours of night spread before them into
endless possibility.

* * *

He'd used her badly. He knew it as he walked from the castle into the freezing waters of the lake. She was a virgin, for God's sake, and he hadn't let her rest 'til the birdsong had pierced the dawn. Even then, he had taken her one last time.

God. What the hell was wrong with him? Grace, trussed in the tumbled linen sheets of whiteness, stained in red.

His seed and her blood.

A virgin no longer.

It was done.

Finished.

He laughed as he surfaced from the deep, primal and free. He was alive like he had never felt alive before, replete with sex, and be damned the consequences of any of it.

For once he did not feel the weight of Malcolm or Ruth's betrayal upon his shoulders.

Bathing, Grace winced at the way her whole body protested against movement, the warm water washing away the stickiness of Lachlan Kerr's seed and the staleness of sex.

Taken. Used. Her hand rested across the taut skin on her stomach. Surely a child must have been conceived after such a night. She closed her eyes and breathed deeply, the small rush of lust fanning the secret places that her husband had touched and known, well, with his manhood and his fingers and his mouth.

Heaven.

She had been there, in the quiet of this night, in the throes of passion, in the whispers as he let her rest and the thrust of power when he did not.

And if she was with child? What then? Would his need be slaked? She shook her head. Nay, he could not just take her for one night. Surely not! The heavy throb of need left its own craving. Lachlan Kerr, his ring on her finger binding her to him, to his smell, his voice, the feel of his skin against hers and the generosity in his careful unleashing of her lust.

Everything felt more…lucid, that was the word, the tense worry of her usual demeanour banished under the finesse of his lovemaking. A flush of heat suffused her body. Lord, when she met her husband again in daylight, would the knowledge of their tryst mark his face?

Or show on hers?

She could not even begin to imagine how it would not. And what would he have made of the scars on her thighs? Even in the darkness she knew he would have felt them though he did not ask, did not in any way linger over the disfigurement.

She smiled and stretched, schooling emotion as she donned a clean shift, and greeted the maid who had brought her the water as she again entered the room.

'Ye are to come down to break the fast, my Lady. The Laird wills it. He has sent me to help ye dress.'

The look in her eyes was kind and Grace saw her visibly relax when she nodded and bade her to stay. Her day gowns were complex and she was used to the ministrations of a maid at Grantley. And today, after last night, she had a need to look her very best.

A tiny frown eclipsed joy as her eyes ran over the red skin

at her elbows. She hoped her face might not have broken out into the same rash, but with no mirror she had to trust in touch only and that seemed to suggest that everything was all right.

'I think the r-r-red gown.' She motioned to the many dresses hanging from wide hooks on the wall. Grace had seldom worn this particular colour, but today with her confidence growing she decided to.

'It is verra braw.'

'Braw?'

'Beautiful, my Lady,' the woman returned.

As beautiful as she was not. All the old uncertainties returned with a force.

'I have changed my mind, I shall wear the blue one.'

This dress was nowhere near as fine, but the maid did as she was bidden, tying the bodice when Grace was in the gown and arranging the pleats across the neckline.

'Would you allow me to dress your hair too, my Lady? Many say that I have considerable skill in that area and it is such a lovely colour.'

Looking at the servant carefully, Grace tried to determine whether or not she jested, but the honesty so easily seen stamped in her eyes told her otherwise.

'What is your name?' she asked.

'Elizabeth is my real name, though to everybody here I am Lizzie.'

'I usually just bind my hair up beneath a wimple, Lizzie…' She had never bothered much with the styles of the day, preferring instead the easy fashion of the older women.

'Oh, no, my lady. I could plait it in a certain way. May I…?' Her hand came out tentatively, threading through the length of redness when Grace inclined her head. 'Ye have such hair. 'Tis like a curtain of fire.'

Fire. In the trees around her as she hid behind the trunk of an oak, moonlight dimmed by flame and the neck of her mother hanging at a strange angle. Cut.

'Are ye all right?' The maid's hand on her arm was cold. 'It seemed ye went somewhere for a moment. Somewhere wicked sad.'

Grace took in breath and tried to find normality. This woman was the first person, save for her husband, who had made any attempt at conversation since she had arrived here in Belridden and she did not want to frighten her away.

'Perhaps, after all, I should like to have my hair dressed,' she said and sat on the stool by the bed.

Lizzie looked relieved as she brought a brush from her ample pouch. 'When I have finished, I will bring ye a hand mirror so that ye can see how well ye look.'

When Grace walked into the Great Hall, the conversation of those all around ceased momentarily, the silence worrying her as she stepped up to the top table. The chair beside her husband was empty and she sat, rearranging her generous skirts until she finally gained the courage to look her husband in the eyes.

The detached and careless way he looked back suggested none of the emotion of less than a few hours ago and even when his focus shifted to the way her hair was fashioned she could detect not the slightest glimmer of regard.

He neither stood at her entry nor helped her with the placement of her chair. Nay, he sat there with his pale, pale eyes and watched with an implacable and unmoving stillness.

'You are late. Do not be so again.' With that he lifted his knife and began to cut his bread, plying it with thick curd cheese and a handful of cold meat.

The space between their chairs was like a widening chasm.

'The m-maid did my hair. It t-t-took some time.'

His eyes glanced up. 'I preferred it as it was.'

'Unbound?'

'Yes.' Short and staccato. A careless indifference.

'It is ina-a-appropriate for a married woman to wear her h-hair loose.'

'And appropriate is important to you?' An undercurrent of anger was so barely hidden that she had no idea how to respond. Was he alluding to her behaviour last night? Wanton. Abandoned. Rash.

'It i-is, my Lord.'

Turning away, he spoke with the older woman next to him.

'*Grandmère*. This is Grace Stanton.'

The smile faded in one singular second. 'You loved Malcolm, *n'est pas*? Loved him before…' The old woman extracted a kerchief from her sleeve, dabbing weeping eyes on the thin scrap of lace. 'He was…an adventurer who loved chance and danger, you understand. My wild boy,' she said with a great deal of love and regret. 'I cannot comprehend what happened….'

Her French accent overrode every syllable, as did her sorrow. And in her misgivings lay a great many questions.

'He was a good man, no?'

'I am certain th-that he was.' Grace knotted her hands together on her lap beneath the table.

'And you loved him?'

Not trusting the words that could come, she merely nodded. *Lies. Lies. Lies.*

'He gave her the Kerr ring.' Her husband dug in his sporran and retrieved the treasure before laying it on the table where it sat like a witness to falsity, its sparkling red mocking Grace's every single truthless utterance.

'Then he must have been happy…' The rush of sobs brought forth the old lady's maid and she was helped from the seat and out of the hall.

Lachlan Kerr watched her for a moment, his fingers striking the table before him in a restless beat. 'You know, for the life of me I cannae see my brother and you—' He stopped and reached out for the ring, turning it as he took breath. 'Malcolm was my grandmother's favourite. And my father's. So he was spoiled, I suppose. He got his way in things more often then he should have. If he did anything to hurt you…'

'He did not.' Strident, definitive, the tear-stained face of Ginny and the furious anger of Stephen lending her voice an edge that she could never have feigned.

'Then I am glad of it.' Replacing the ring, he sliced himself another crust of bread and reached out for the salt and mustard. The knife he used was engraved with his initials in the horn of the bone. L.M.K. She wondered what the M stood for.

Malcolm? Like his brother? Perhaps it was a family name. How close had they been, for there was only thirteen months between them? She remembered Stephen telling her that after they had prayed together in the chapel at Grantley on the evening that Malcolm Kerr had fallen. Were they seeking absolution? She had certainly not felt it in all of the three hundred or so days since.

Yet Lachlan Kerr had not come with the others sent from Belridden to understand just where it was that the accident had happened, nor had he replied to the message her uncle had sent explaining his demise.

Why had he stayed so distant? she wondered, the thought interrupted as he spoke.

'Today the castle will be prepared for a celebration of our nuptials.'

'B-But n-no one looks pleased about me being here.'

'A good meal and fine wine will alleviate things, and when I repair the cottars' roofs with your gold, they will be happier still.'

Just the dowry, then! All the hopes from last night's loving were dashed, though, catching his eyes, she was shocked as a white-hot bolt of awareness flooded between them. Unexpected. He turned away as if he had been burned and the look on his face was hardly happy.

'You still pine for my dead brother and I have lost the ability to believe in anything at all. Do not imagine this union of ours is something that it is not.'

Grace felt her body choke at his honesty and she made herself look down, unable to remain aloof from the pain of his rejection and wanting to hide her easily read expression.

And beneath her skirt the places that his body had awoken beat with a growing rhythm.

Take me.

Again.

Pulsating with the hopeless echo of longing.

She leaned over slightly as she picked up her knife and the feel of his arm against hers heightened everything. When he pulled back, she resisted leaning further. The smell of lye soap and male was heady and when she looked across at his wrists, the same thin lines that she had noticed before fascinated her. She knew little of Lachlan Kerr's history, little of his first wife or his subsequent liaisons.

All she truly knew of her husband was the way that her body responded to his touch… Stop it, she chastised herself, the quiet edge of reason protecting her from his distance.

When the woman, Rebecca, walked into the hall, she saw how her husband gestured to the empty seat beside him and saw also how he smiled in welcome, his hand against the other woman's arm, the long blonde curtain of her hair falling, unbound, thick, silky. Like hers was not.

She suddenly regretted the fussy style of her own hair and, looking around the room, observed the way those on the benches watched her, with a great deal of caution and an even greater deal of dislike. She was a plain interloper with the stigma of a Kerr death attached to her name, and now the second wife to a man who plied his mistress with favours whilst she sat there looking on. Rebecca McInness's fingers wandered between Lachlan's legs. Lewd and patently visible, the material of her bodice had fallen almost to the line of her nipples. He made no move to stop her brazenness, either, but took another glass of ale.

Unsteadily she stood. 'I f-f-find after all that I am n-n-not hungry.' Pointedly she placed her clean napkin down.

Her husband, however, was not letting her go so easily. 'I have given you no leave to retire.'

'H-Have you not?' The catch in her voice negated the whole effect of haughtiness and the smile on the face of his mistress undermined it yet again.

The hall had quietened at this unexpected exchange. Still she could not find it in herself to retreat, but stood there, caught between anger and embarrassment and distress.

'Sit down.'

She shook her head, but did not move and was debating what to do when a scream sounded from the kitchen and a child erupted from a doorway, the edge of his tunic well on fire.

Two steps and she had him in her arms, the generous cloth of her skirt wrapped around the flames and the jug of ale on the table dousing everything.

Fire. Flames. The child's shocked brown eyes, his mother's running steps and pain. In her hands and up her arms and in the tight recess of memory.

Pain. Like before.

Her legs buckled beneath her and she staggered towards

the only man who had ever been vaguely kind to her outside her own kin. Lachlan Kerr's frown was deep as he caught her before she fell.

Hot. She was too hot.

'Water.' Had she said it? She tried again.

'Be still, Grace.' His voice through layers of grey and then hands on her brow. Cool. Steady. Liquid dripped into her mouth. Sweet.

There was darkness behind him, and the candlelight held the two of them trapped in a ring of flame.

Flame. 'The child…?'

'Was burned a lot less severely than you were.' Impatient. Worried.

The room was one that she did not recognise and she hated the tears that fell across her cheeks. When she raised up her hands to stop them, the heavy bandages surprised her.

'The housekeeper applied a poultice of her own making.'

'And my face?'

He traced one thumb over her cheek and brow. 'Was not harmed.'

'Wh-wh-who was he?'

'The child?'

She nodded and waited for him to tell her.

'Connor's oldest boy, Donald. He has asked after you every day.'

'Every day?'

'You have had the fever for almost a week now. We thought at first you would nae survive it.'

That explained the exhaustion she felt and the easy tears. Lachlan Kerr looked worse for wear as well, thick stubble on his cheeks and chin and dark rings beneath his eyes. Cloth wound around his left hand made her frown.

'From my attempt at quelling the flames on your sleeves,' he explained when he saw where it was she looked. 'Donald had tipped over a pan of fat drippings and it was difficult to extinguish.'

'Thank you.' His grip tightened and even with layers of cloth between them heat blazed.

Quickly she looked away. He had made it clear to her the sort of relationship that he wished between them.

Still, she was alone here at Belridden and his friendship was important. Swallowing down her pride, she tried to smile. 'Your mistress is v-very beautiful.'

He did not answer.

'And I—I am s-sorry that it was m-me you h-had to m-marry. I c-could have stopped it.'

His attention was firmly caught. 'How?'

'My uncle gave m-me the ch-choice of entering a nunnery or m-marrying you.'

God! Her eyes in this light were full of tears and for the first time Lachlan understood just what this marriage must have cost her. All humour fled.

'As a novice you would have been expected to stay in your chosen holy order for the rest of your life.'

Another tear traced its way down her cheek. 'P-Perhaps I sh-should have listened to him….'

'No.' He meant what he said, the memory of their night together surfacing strongly. Bravery had its own allure, and with her dancing red curls vivid against the white of linen, Grace Stanton looked as pretty as he had ever seen her. Plucking a strand from its bed against the feather pillow, he wound it around his thumb.

'The physician insisted on cutting your hair as a precaution against the fever.'

Worry creased her brow and the uncovered ends of her fingers patted at the length. 'Is it too short?'

He laughed and hurt coated her face.

'Even a p-plain woman has a best feature, my Lord.'

'And you think this is yours?'

'I did.'

Simple and straightforward.

Lachlan's heart twisted and he didn't like the feeling. Moving away out of the light, he stood against the fireplace, empty now of flame, to regroup.

All his life he had been surrounded by betrayal and lies and deceit and the pure beauty of truth was a powerful weapon. Too powerful, with his lack of sleep and the shape of her bare body tempting him beneath the thin layer of sheet.

His wife. Grace. Even her name suited her. Could grace be possible after all? He shook his head and wished he had a drink in hand, the deep burn on his fingers hurting like hell.

Outside he could hear the keening winds fresh off the

Cheviots. Soon it would be autumn. He splayed his damaged skin out against the coldness of the stone.

Nay, grace wasn't possible for a man like him, an unbeliever, a Kerr. The curse on his family wound itself around everything, even repentance.

When he turned again to his wife, he saw she watched him, her eyes soft brown and knowing. The smile he gave her back was forced and it faltered somewhat as she spoke.

'There is o-one more thing I w-w-w-would like to know?'

He nodded, hoping the question would not concern his brother, not here with her hurt, and lies all he could give her back.

'Is b-bedding your m-mistress always as wondrous as it w-was with me?'

'It is not.'

'Th-then I am g-glad for it.'

And with that she closed her eyes and fell asleep, the rhythm of her breath more even than it had been and a hint of laughter on her lips.

Wondrous? He scuffed at the floor and swallowed back misgiving. He could never remember Rebecca even once making his heart race with the speed it did when bedding Grace.

And she had known. He had seen the look in his wife's eyes as she had asked the question, hooded and sensual, which made it all so much worse.

Uncertainty welled. She was not quite the pious woman she claimed to be, then, and a niggle of question worried at him.

Chapter Six

The pain in her hands had lessened by the morning as she sat on the side of the bed and watched Lizzie tidy the room.

'Ye've been the talk of the castle, my Lady, what with your burns and your bravery and I'll be hearing none of your denials about it.'

Grace smiled. 'Is my husband already eating his morning meal?'

'Your husband? Nay, did ye not ken he has ridden north on the orders of the king?'

'North?'

'To Edinburgh and the council of the chiefs. Our Laird has the ear of King David and he uses him often as a voice of reason. He was with him, ye ken, in France as a child and then again in Hampshire for a time after the Battle of Neville's Cross in '46.'

Grace frowned. If Lachlan and his king were so close, why had David insisted on this match with her? Nothing quite made sense. The fact that he had not even come to say goodbye also rankled. Still, at least he had been honest with his admission of feelings. He had none. And so of course he would not tarry to give her the news of his plans. A new thought surfaced. 'Is there a looking glass I could use, Lizzie?' Her hand came up to the unfamiliar shortness of her hair, heavy curls bouncing around the side of her face and not even grazing the neckline of her shift.

'Indeed there is.' Placing pan and broom on the floor, she scurried away, returning less than a moment later with a disc of polished copper, its handle softened with fine leather strips.

'We will put it here, and ye can keep it in this room. It should have come in last week, but what with the burns and fuss and everything it was forgotten. Can ye see yourself in the reflection?'

Grace nodded, speechless at the returned image. Her hair was different, glossier, thicker, and redder if it could possibly have been so.

'I think it suits ye, my Lady, and the ointment the physician made up has been applied to your arms. The raised skin seems much lessened.'

Joy welled. For years she had been trying different potions, various mixtures and tinctures and medicines to counteract the itchiness, and all to no avail. But here at Belridden, in the unlikeliest of all places, a cure might have finally been found. She could barely contain her excitement. 'Would he make me up some more of the ointment, do you think?'

'Nay, he does not have to do that. He left me with the instructions, ye see. Helmet-flower and monkshood mixed with comfrey and the hips of roses. I was the one who boiled up this pot.'

Grace turned again to the mirror, tilting her head this way and that, the wide smile reflected making her laugh out aloud.

'I've never liked to look at myself much, Lizzie, so I am sorry if today I appear so vain…'

'Och, ye are the least vain lady I've ever met and I won't have ye saying anything of the sort.'

'I just can't believe my hair has become so curly.'

'It was the weight of the length of it before that held it down. Had it never been cut?'

'No. The healer at Grantley said if I did so I could risk more skin problems and my mother's hair was always very long.'

'Did she mind ye going so far from home? Your mother, I mean?'

'She passed away years ago, just before my father did.'

'Then I am sorry for it.'

Grace suddenly had another thought. 'How did the Laird's f-first wife die?'

A heavy frown marred Lizzie's forehead. 'Ruth Kerr died after the birth of her child.'

'There is a child?'

'There was a child, stillborn and buried with her mother in the cemetery by the western wall. Some say that your husband poisoned her.'

'And you? What d-do you say?'

The maid's pursed lips spoke more tellingly than any words and Grace knew that she would speak no more about it.

She spent the next afternoon in the small chapel at Belridden, enjoying its silence and beauty and puzzled by the fact that no one else at all came to pray. Was it reserved for the Laird and his family? Everything about the place looked…unused: the pews, the altar, the benches covered in a thin layer of dust. There were no boot marks or scratches, no air of use. Instead, the dust motes swirled in the light of coloured glass, slow, languid and undisturbed until she had come.

A small cough made her turn and the boy who had been burned in the Great Hall was waiting at the doorway. He bowed low when he saw that she had seen him. 'When ye are finished, my Lady, I have something for ye.' He did not put one foot across the lintel.

Genuflecting and whispering a quick prayer, Grace left the chapel, the sunlight bright after the dim inside.

'You are Donald?'

'I am, my Lady, and I wanted to thank you for helping me…'

His face was red and Grace smiled, trying to put him at ease. Instead he blushed even brighter.

'It's this way.' He gestured to a track visible between a hedgerow, twenty yards away.

Looking up at the castle, Grace saw that the guards watched them. Surely it should be safe to follow the boy a little way? With a nod she slipped in behind him and into the shadow of the trees.

It was a good two hundred yards until he stopped, the face of a low cliff before her with an opening about three feet wide. Wildflowers grew at the entrance, the windless warmth of shelter keeping them colourful and thick.

'It's in here, my Lady.'

Stepping in, she was amazed. No small insignificant cave this, but an enormous light-filled grotto with water running to one side. Bunches of the same flowers outside had been picked and placed in two chipped pottery tankards and a naïvely fashioned picture done on cloth of the Holy Family was nailed to the wall between them.

A natural chapel. One of light and water and warmth.

'Me mam said that you liked to pray so I made you a place to do it. No one goes in the chapel you see, not since—' He stopped. And stood very still.

'Not since…?'

'The old Laird died in it, my Lady, after the priest gave a curse.' His lips tightened and he looked around as if someone else could be listening, as if the oath of which he spoke had been a recent thing.

'How old are you, Donald?'

'I'll be ten in November at Samhain, and you dinna stammer when you talk to me like I heard you do in the Great Hall.'

She smiled, the truth of what he said so surprising. 'Perhaps it is this place, then. Do others come here?'

'Och, there a hundred other caves and not so far, so this one is mostly mine. I brought you something else as well. For luck.' He dug into his pocket and retrieved a rock.

Holding it in her hand, Grace saw that it had been cut in half and the plane had been polished, the shape of an insect caught complete in amber, as if in an instant its life had been frozen.

'It's an argus moth and d-double banded.'

Grace remembered Ginny being as interested in the natural world as this boy was when she was young, and the thought was comforting as she listened. If her cousin ever came to this place, she would one day show her these things, these treasures, for there had been a time when she had enjoyed walking the hills and looking—

She stopped and pushed down anger.

Malcolm Kerr had seen an end to that. Now Ginny rarely left the confines of Grantley and always within the company of others. Nervous. Inward. Mute.

A great well of homesickness washed across her. How long would it be until she could ever go home?

Home?

Belridden was home now, with a husband who tolerated her only because she would provide an heir. More than one! She suddenly saw herself as an older woman with a bitter heart and knew that she wanted much more. She wanted life and love and happiness, for otherwise she would be trapped like this insect, for ever in amber.

A shout had them both turning and when they walked outside the cave Connor was there, dusty from a ride, and astonished to see her with his young son.

'If he has been bothering ye at all…'

'No. H-He has b-been showing m-me treasures.'

'Your mam wants ye home, Donald. Now.'

When the boy scampered off he watched him, the lithe legs running free.

'He is our first-born. A little wild, perhaps, but with a good heart.'

Grace nodded and pocketed the amber.

'My wife and I both thank ye for saving him and I know ye have burns yourself from doing so.'

'They are almost gone.' She held up her hands, the bandages lighter now and the pain much alleviated, though the man opposite still glowered at the sight.

'The Laird sat wi' ye through the nights, d'ye ken, for he would nae let another do it.' He hesitated before going on. 'There is much said of Lachlan Kerr that is unfair. He is a good man who deserves a good woman. I hope that is you.'

Important words, given as a gift in exchange for the one she had given him. Lachlan's soldier would not talk like this with her again. Grace knew it to the very marrow of her bones, and knew too that if she did not take advantage of his confidence she would be sorry.

'I have h-heard my h-husband poisoned h-his first wife?'

'From whom did ye hear that?'

She offered nothing.

'There are people in this castle, my Lady, who could be dangerous to you, but on my word, Lachlan Kerr is not one of them.'

'Thank you.' Simple. Said.

When he tipped his head and walked away she did not follow, but stood beneath the cliff in the sun, watching small flying insects cross over beams of light and shadow, gliding free.

The Laird sat wi' ye through the nights, d'ye ken, for he would nae let another do it.

She pulled the amber from her pocket and rubbed the polished face. Just for luck.

* * *

Lachlan was tired of being in Edinburgh, tired of the intrigue and the conspiracy and the careful way of words. But most of all he was tired of the women who crowded about him seeking favour.

It had always been like this, he ruminated, and he had always enjoyed it. But this time things were different. He wondered how Grace was and if her hands were healed or if his seed had taken.

God, even the thought of it had him rising, here in the court of his king and in the middle of the day.

And David and his English sympathies weren't helping any either. Scottish independence had been hard won by the Bruce and for David to be even thinking of a treaty to place an Englishman on the Scottish throne was bound to lead to rebellion. Sometimes he barely recognised the man from the boy he had always known, the student who could recite the Declaration of Arbroath word for word.

Sir John Murray from Bothwell Castle sat beside him in a room off the stone keep behind the Chapel of St Margaret.

'It seems that captivity in England has softened David's head.'

Lachlan finished the fine tumbler of French wine and looked over his shoulder to see who else was close. Ideas like this could be construed as scheming should they be overheard by the wrong ears.

'Well, it wasna' us in confinement under English rule for nigh on eleven years, aye, John, and who's to know what that would do to a man? But I'd be thinking that, if the regional magnates get the true gist of what he's planning, we'll have rebellion in the streets.'

'And on the estates.'

Lach nodded. 'The trouble is David's ideas were never formed here in Scotland, never settled long enough to make the bonds, and the merks from the Berwick Treaty are nae helping anything either. Two payments and then what, for the nobles are stretched enough already with their own debts.'

Both men looked across at the king.

The liabilities of money, a fragile economy and an ineffective king were no mix for a strong Scotland. Again Lachlan wished that he was home.

'If he had an heir, it might all be different.'

John's face suddenly lit up with interest. 'Speaking of which—'

Lachlan interrupted him, knowing where it was he was going with such a question. 'I had been married less than two weeks before David pulled me up here.'

'And ye now want to go back?'

The laughter in his friend's face unnerved him as did the kernel of truth in his words.

'Ye've done enough for the King of Scots, Lachlan, with all the years ye were away in France at the Chateau-Gaillard and at Odiham in Hampshire. Perhaps it's time now to get your own house in order, aye?'

From any other man Lachlan would have taken the advice as an affront, but he had known John Murray longer even than he had known David and the counsel would be given with the best of intentions.

Belridden rose up like a ruined heartstone, pulling at him, the Kerr blood spilled on its soil for centuries. When he had married Ruth he thought that he would not leave it again and yet, with her melancholy and the negotiations for David's release, he had been away far more than he had ever been home.

Perhaps, then, what had happened next was not all her fault; perhaps some of the blame belonged to him, an absent husband who had been too long at war and a man who could never brook the ties that family wound around him.

The introspection worried him and he stood.

'I had heard that ye will be journeying south in the next weeks?'

'Aye.'

'Be sure then to call in at my keep.'

'To meet your wife?'

Lachlan said nothing as he left.

He returned at sunset to Belridden on the tenth day after he had left it and he returned to chaos.

The fire had started in the mill in the early morning and there were still plumes where hot spots had not been quite doused. But it was neither the loss of food stores nor the ruin of the building that most worried him. Nay, it was the fact that a woman had been seen just before the fire had taken hold. A woman with a hooded dark blue woollen cloak and fine black shoes.

Grace.

Connor tried to explain it to him even as he was dismounting from his horse.

'Tom the old cottar saw this figure when he was out with his dogs and Bridget the smith's daughter saw her, too, running for the glade behind the western wall.'

'Just the figure, not the face? It could have been anyone.'

Connor was silent for a few seconds, as though considering what he would say. 'Many in the castle believe that it was your wife.'

'I see. Where is my wife?'

'In her room. She has not left it since being asked about the fire.'

Passing the reins of his horse to a stable hand, Lach dusted himself down. After a long ride this was the last thing he needed, but he did not want to leave the suppositions festering any longer. As he walked there was a strange silence in the Great Hall, as if the place held its breath, waiting to see what would happen next. Even Rebecca, wiping the tables by the fireplace, kept her distance.

Grace was sitting by the window, the shutters pulled and her hair wild curly red around her shoulders.

For a second he found himself thinking how much more she suited it this length, but then her eyes came up to his, swollen and fearful. The room was very cold.

'I d-d-did not d-do it.'

When she stood, he saw she now wore only a light bandage on one hand.

'Do you have a hooded blue cloak?'

'Y-yes.'

'Is it still in your possession?'

She nodded and opened a chest beside her, watching as he strode to take the garment out. No smell of flame or smoke. No charcoal or ash or grass stains.

'If you are blameless, no one will hurt you.'

She shook her head and he heard the word 'if' repeated.

'I th-th-thought they were b-beginning to like m-me.'

He had to smile at her innocence. God, even as a youngster he had not had the same measure of it.

'I th-thought you would come b-back and see that they l-liked me, your p-people.'

'And that would be important to you because…?' He could not quite fathom where she was going with this reasoning, the stain in her cheeks deepening as a maid came in through the opened door.

'I am so sorry, my Lord, I hadna realised that ye had come home and I thought to help your wife dress for dinner.'

'You will come down, then?'

'I d-did not d-do it. Why should I not eat?'

Anger laced the brown of Grace's eyes and Lach felt a quick rush of passion. It was well past a fortnight since he had lain with her. If he had been sure that she would not fight him, he would have dismissed the servant then and there and taken her to bed. He swallowed back need and turned away, the present he had brought her from Edinburgh still in his pouch.

It was a clip for her hair from the city of Constantinople. He had seen it in the shop window in the narrow closes behind the castle and procured it immediately, an impulsive reckless buy that had cost him far too many coins.

His fingers closed over the smoothness of the shell as he left the room.

That evening a celebration was held for his safe return from Edinburgh and the Great Hall was as full as he had seen it, cottars coming up from the village for the feast and the benches overflowing with curiosity and with downright dislike.

For Grace.

Lachlan knew he should have moved away from his wife, but with the mood of his people so unreadable he found that he just could not.

Tonight she was dressed in a gown that made her look every inch the lady that she was born to be, the red brocade train matching a ruby necklace around her throat, and it was this obvious show of wealth that seemed to be the problem. No woman here could compete with the opulence and no man could understand the need to show off such grandeur, especially with the accusation of being the fire starter so clearly palpable. So she placed herself in a no man's land between suspicion and overindulgence, the steeple hat she wore rising a good three feet in the air, the wired contraption itself an interloper from the far-off world of courts and kings.

If she had been fairer of face or more tractable, she might have got away with it, but she wasn't. The skin on her neck was roughened again tonight, and what could be seen of her hair clashed against the lighter colour of the cloth. He swiped his own hair back and schooled growing irritation, for he knew now that gleam in his wife's eyes. Fright over-laced with bravery and a dollop of challenge.

Rebecca's laughter was not helping either, or the fact that she had chosen almost the exact same shade of gown as his wife by some canny misfortune. A good number of his men crowded around his mistress, plying her with the ale he had had brought up from the cellars. Grace, on the other hand, refused libation and sat like one who did not welcome any company but her own.

'If you would like a dance, Con has the way of the steps.'

For the first time that evening she faced him.

'I d-doubt very much that he w-would wish to dance w-with me.'

The raucous shouts of those who milled around Rebecca filled the room.

'I give you l-leave to go if you want to join h-her—'

He did not let her finish. 'Nay, I think you are the one who needs protecting tonight.'

Her eyes flinted and she swallowed. 'W-was much l-lost in the f-fire?'

'Flour. Sacks. The wooden water wheel.'

'My dowry could replace these things.'

'Sometimes money is not always a solution, and any re-placement of what you claim to have no knowledge of in the first place may be construed as guilt.'

'I did not m-mean…'

'Whoever started the fire will be caught and punished.'

'As they sh-should be,' she answered and wound a red-shot silk gauze scarf around her hand. Lachlan remembered doing the same the night he had taken her virginity. The ties he had used had been burgundy, and her skin almost translucent beneath it.

God, was she a witch perhaps, this wife of his, entangling lust with need and to hell with sense or reason? He checked the position of the moon in the sky through an open shutter, and saw it was late. When Rebecca caught his glance from the other side of the room, he looked away and thought nothing of her chagrin. Nay, Grace took all of his concentration.

'Are ye with child from our time together?'

Her tongue traced a line around her lips, the buds of her nipples stretched taut against the fabric of her dress. The tight lust he felt annoyed him.

'I th-think it is too soon t-to tell.'

Her tone was self-conscious and, with her curls dancing around her face, she looked much younger than the twenty-six years she professed. 'The length of your hair suits you, aye.' His hands stiffened against the line of his thighs as he wondered what the hell had made him say that and when she reached up the freckles on the back of her hand were so different to the blemish-free white skin of his mistress.

Hell. Had his life come down to comparing Grace with every other woman he had ever known intimately and giving compliments when he found the others wanting? Irritation made him unkind.

'As my wife, one of your duties is to oversee the running

of this place. Tomorrow I shall have the housekeeper show you just what is involved.'

'I sh-should be h-happy to.'

'If you leave the castle, make certain you take one of my soldiers with you.'

'So they can s-see that I should not bring h-harm to your keep?'

He laughed and the sound was rusty.

'I had not thought of it in quite that way.' This time her eyes met his directly and the candlelight fired the amber to a different shade of brown. 'More for protection.'

'Against w-what?'

Lachlan looked across at her. How easy and safe the living in England must have been for her even to have to ask him such. Here nothing was secure. Neither home nor hearth nor country.

'This is Scotland, Grace, and you play a dangerous game with all your questions, but if you value your head it would be wiser to keep it down and out of trouble.'

When she nodded gravely, the dimples in her cheeks deeply etched in thought, he felt his physical want for her intensify. God in Heaven, nothing made sense. He looked across the room to Rebecca and was vexed by her childish pout and bad temper. All he wanted was Grace. He could not find it in himself to even be careful.

'Will you lie with me again tonight?'

The gold in her eyes sparked, a mirror of his own lust. 'Y-you are my husband. You c-can take me when you will it.'

'And where,' he returned fast, all semblance of manners lost under want and need. Her. In her. Entering into the softness of womanhood and seeing her curls jolt with the movement.

She nodded, even to that, though she did not look at him directly.

'I will meet you in your room, then, after I have spoken with Connor.'

She bowed her head and departed, the sway of her hips distracting him from Con's words as he watched her go, threading her way through the crowd of people with her head held high and conversing with no one.

Grace took off her fine dress and the tall hat with the veil that tumbled in a light fall of cloth from its peak. But she did not remove her garters holding the stockings and reaching the junction between her thighs, or the ruby necklace gleaming bright from her throat. Lord, how glad she was to be away from the hall below and from the falsetto laugh of Rebecca McInness.

Repairing to her bed, she arranged herself upon it, and when the door opened and Lachlan Kerr entered she did not look away.

'*Merci aux saints,*' he enunciated, dropping the slats behind him and crossing the room in three easy footfalls. Cupping her unclothed buttock with his right hand, he shrugged off his shirt with the left, the hardness of him making her smile until he bundled the length of her hair around his fist.

'When I cover you this time, my Lady, I intend to have you begging me to stop.'

'Starting now,' she answered back, biting into the skin at his wrist and crying out as they came together, the pure and sheer rightness of it freeing.

'The candles,' she said raggedly, as he rocked her hips up to his, 'I w-want them out.'

Wetting his fingers, he extinguished the glare.

They lay together spent, her body draped over his and her hair wildly tangled, rising up and down with the heaviness of his breath.

She was a temptress. Pure and simple. His plain and timid wife was a woman of unequalled sensuality. Bringing his hand up from the sheet, he laid it across her back, carefully so that she would not wake.

Grace. Asleep. He noticed the light fall of her breath and a perfume he could not recognise. Flowers of some sort, he reasoned. It was in her skin and in her hair. And for the first time ever after making love to a woman he did not want to rise and leave, the feel of her curled body within his own right somehow.

He listened to the last shouts from the Great Hall and was glad that he was not down there, glad that he was in this bed with his wife in his arms and the door well sealed against any intrusion.

This wife.

So unlike the last one.

So unlike any other woman he had ever shared a bed with, and, truth be told, there had been many.

His glance wandered to the gartered stockings slung carelessly on to the rush mat, stockings he had removed some-where after midnight when she begged him not to stop.

How had she come by the injuries on her thighs? His grip tightened. The marks that fire left? Certainty blurred into question.

Feeling the movement of her lashes against his chest, he knew that she had awakened and yet she stayed as silent as he did, enjoying the last moments of togetherness before reality wrenched them apart.

How well had she loved his brother? How much did she know of his death? Was there any credence in the circulat-ing rumours that laid the blame for Malcolm's disappear-ance squarely at her feet?

These were questions that he needed to ask. But not now. Not when the rush of sex came upon him again and he turned, liking the way her body wrapped about his before she accepted him in.

Chapter Seven

Grace walked along the castle path early the next afternoon. Today a haze fell across the land, gentling it and
giving it a wild sort of beauty that England lacked, the
stone of Belridden taking on almost a pinkish hue. The tall
starkness of it looked less ugly, a keep designed for defence,
and in this world far from civilisation, safety had its own
particular allure.

Safety. Her fists balled by her side as she remembered
last night, remembered the passion between them, raw and
undisciplined, all resistance gone in a sheer and over-
whelming response. Even now she could still feel her excitement of it, the wonder and the intensity, and the
protection.

Tears came to her eyes, welling up and threatening to fall.
She would always be safe here, cocooned in the title of
wife, with the nights of many years lining up before her.
Would he come again tonight? Her lips turned up at the
thought, for the bud of a woman's power was forming and
she could see her husband atop a palfrey and riding towards

her from the woodland behind the water meadow. This horse was smaller than the one he had come to England on and the bridle was coloured in the reds and greens of the Kerr clan, a chevron in the same shades embossed on his saddle. Not only a Laird but a knight and he had brought his badge with him from the court of Philip.

The mill was a burnt-out shell, its waterwheel hanging in charred lines across the river, and he was not looking pleased. Her elation was dampened further when a retainer joined him, suspicion in his eyes as they met her own.

'We'll need to rebuild before winter, Laird. The wheel and roof are completely lost and much of the corn in from the fields gone with it.'

'Bring men to clear away the beams and cut new timber from the forest. Then promise bread from the castle kitchens and the free use of the woods for game in return for worked hours.'

Grace listened with a growing regard for her husband's logic and good sense as he outlined plans to get the mill running again. Finally he seemed satisfied with what they would do and, farewelling his soldier, he dismounted. It was cold and she wished that she had worn her cloak, but with all the conjecture about a woman in blue she did not dare be seen out in it. She was amazed at how little her husband had on in this weather, his highland shirt open at the collar and his legs bare. In the light of a new day all that had happened in the darkness between them seemed unreal, the brittle sharpness of his glance deflating any shared confidences and reducing her to worry.

'I can s-see that people think I d-did this.'

'Well, there hasn'a ever been a fire before at Belridden that's done this amount of damage and you the only stranger here. You must know how it looks from the way of others.'

'A-and if it happens a-again—?'

He broke in. 'Are you saying that it might?'

She shook her head. 'No. But if someone else p-pretends it?'

Anger crossed his brow. 'Then they will be caught.' He was quiet for a moment before he continued. 'If it is you for some reason, Grace, then it would be best to tell me of it now.'

'It was not m-me.' She willed back the pain as she walked beside him, bleakness and desolation replacing hope as they made towards the keep. She could not think he should believe that of her. Perhaps he was more like his brother than she knew.

Her mind went back to the night Malcolm Kerr had arrived in Grantley from London with her cousin. He had taken one look at her and laughed.

'Ye brought me up from court for this woman, Stephen?' He was careful his voice did not carry around the room and that her uncle had no notion of his rudeness. 'I could have married any number of plain heiresses in London and certainly none with the same shade of hair.' His sneer was ripe, and, had there been a cart willing to make the trip back to town that evening, all that had happened next might have been avoided.

For Ginny had walked into the hall with her hair newly washed and a fresh gown of sapphire blue, exactly the same shade as her eyes. Grace had seen the interest on the face of her would-be suitor and something in her had turned. Something frightening.

She shook her head. Lachlan Kerr was nothing like his brother, but today he was distant and distracted, the careful lover of the night replaced in daylight by a man with plenty on his mind. Her glance took in his fingers laced through the bridle reins, fingers that had caressed her body with magic. She smiled at her nonsensical thoughts, glad that he had no way of reading her mind, though his next observation worried her.

'You are quiet this morning?'

What did that mean? Was he comparing her demeanour today with that of last night? Her humour completely disappeared. Of course he was not thinking such a thing. Why, he had barely noticed her, save to ask if she had knowledge of the fire, and he was certainly keeping a good space between them.

'It m-must be a lot of r-responsibility to be Laird,' she chanced, scratching at a spot at her wrist.

'Does the burn still trouble you?' he asked and unexpectedly reached out to take her arm, bringing the hand up into a better line of vision.

She tried to snatch it away. 'Nay, it is gone. How l-long have you b-been the Laird?' She asked the question more out of the hope of distraction.

'Since Malcolm died.'

Ten months. So it was not long. She was pleased when he let her fingers go.

'M-my uncle often said it t-took a brave man to go into b-battle and a b-braver one to stay and w-work the land.'

He laughed, the sound ringing in the air, and a sound that she thought he had not much practice in.

'Perhaps he was right. Malcolm was certainly away from Belridden for as many months as he could manage. Did you meet him first in London?'

'N-No. He came to Grantley w-with Stephen.'

'Your cousin? The man who came to Belridden with my brother's things after…?'

He left the question hanging and she looked around. Pale blue eyes bored into her own.

'After the h-horse threw him,' she finished, her nails digging into the soft flesh on her palm. Lord, after last night lying was infinitely harder, reserve and restraint replaced by the knowledge of a kinder man.

There was something, too, in the way he frowned that suggested disbelief in her story. Stephen had said the same when he had returned from Belridden all those months ago and the surprise that had accompanied the offer of Lachlan Kerr's hand in marriage had been underlined with fear that this other brother might have guessed, might know…

Again she shook away the thought.

No one knew, no one save the man who had tumbled head over heels into the depths of the Grantley gully, never to be seen again.

Shouts in the language of Gaelic from the castle wall brought her abruptly from her reverie. Two men on horses were coming from the direction of the village, the clothes they wore telling Grace that they were probably English. Her heart began to thump. Was her family safe? Had something happened to her cousins or her uncle?

'Who are th-they?'

Lach shaded his eyes with the back of his hand. 'Friends,' he answered finally and raised his own hand in greeting.

Lachlan stood with his back to the fire as he tried to understand what he had never thought to hear.

'I saw your brother's missing servant this last month in one of the taverns in London, Lach, drinking more than he should have by all accounts and losing a grand lot of gold on the cards.'

'Kenneth MacIndoe? And you are certain that it was he?'

'I walked straight up to him and slapped him on the back. Said that you were on the look out for him and would appreciate some answers on the death of your brother. When I told him of your marriage, he cursed you on the name of your wife somewhat wicked, and was all in a swivet as he left the hall. I couldnae find him after that, though the tavern master said he had been around a while.'

Lachlan tried to find reason in the man's behaviour. Why would he be hiding in London if there was nothing to conceal, and if any story other than the one circulated of his brother's death became public property, how would this affect Grace? She had loved Malcolm. Still did, perhaps.

The web of deceit and consequences reached around him, tangling him in the lies that he had told, and his hand tightened on the handle of his sword. If laws and kings could fasten one knot, then steel could untie another. It was simple and he had never trusted Kenneth MacIndoe. The story worried him. Gold had its own way of leaving trails and a man with a family waiting for him in the Borderlands had no business to be laying low in a London tavern. Unless…

He shook his head and refused to think on politics. Unbidden, his glance went to the daylight outside. At least seven hours until dusk. Seven hours until he could take his wife again without the questions that a daytime tryst might have engendered. He cursed the length of it and cursed also his own damnable needs, mounting with every second he was not in her, not feeling her hands in places on his body that no woman had ever touched. Sweet. Hot. Generous.

Sending the newcomers for food and drink from the Great Hall, he wiped his hair back from his face and ordered his retainers to the field where the quintain stood, reasoning that a bout of hard work might excise the demons that were growing within him.

By dinnertime his irritation was still not assuaged, the bruises from many hours of heavy fighting practice just underpinning a deeper ache. Rebecca was working on a tapestry on the corner seat by the fire when he summoned her. Stripping off her clothes, he brought her to his bed, the heavy furs of the coverlet soft against their skin as he began the mating dance.

'I thought ye would nae return to me, *a luaidh*.'

'Shh.' He did not want to hear her voice, not now, not with the sound of another in his ears. Burning want. Rebecca's hands were cold and the perfume on her skin was strongly pungent. Not flowers!

Turning her over, he cupped the roundness of her bottom, the silk of corn-white hair outlining her back.

Beautiful. She was beautiful, pale against his brownness and unmarked, the lustre of candlelight radiant on her skin.

Blowing out the flames, he felt her surprise, for always they had copulated where they might look on one another. And enjoy. And when the early evening shadow was not enough, he closed his eyes. Another difference. Better. The blood lust that had been his companion all day had fuller rein now.

Almost right.

But not quite. He swore as the sense of urgency dimmed and his body softened.

Grace saw them leave his room together as she went down to dinner. Lachlan made no effort at all to acknowledge her as they went past, though he did separate himself from the woman as they came into the main hall and Rebecca McInness took her place on the benches as Grace made her way to the top table.

A small victory. A hollow prize. She wished that dinner would be over and she could escape back to her room, away from the stares and glares and questions. Tonight her gown was one of midnight blue, the sleeves slashed from shoulder to wrist to show the paler lining beneath and her hair unbound. Just as her husband liked it!

Lord. Her hands pulled the length forwards and she

plaited it into one tight braid, securing the end into the raised collar of her gown.

When his flinted pale eyes met her own, she glared back, no quarter given to manners or propriety.

'Have you c-caught your fire-starter yet, or have you been too busy?' She was so furious she almost forgot to stutter, and the small glimmer of wariness in his eyes irritated her further.

'Too busy,' he returned before finishing a large draught of strong ale.

The many servants bustled in with platters of meat as he signalled them and he cut a wide crust of bread. 'There was something found in the embers of the mill that was interesting…'

Lifting her eyebrows, Grace waited.

'When did you last wear the brooch you have of a rose fashioned in gold?'

She had not seen it in days, since the very first moments of being here at Belridden, since the bath she had taken before the night they…

'It w-was found there?'

'At the edge of the flames and is still intact, should ye wish for it back?'

'No.' Shades of distrust were heard in his words. The cloak, the shoes and now the brooch. 'S-someone has gone to a l-lot of trouble to m-make me look guilty.'

'Indeed.' His voice was low as if, given the seriousness of such an accusation, he wanted what was said to stay between them. She knew that it could not be like this for long, not with the clues stacking up against her. Looking down the table, she noticed how Connor watched her, and Ian. And further away on the benches she caught the worried glance of Lizzie. She had one person in her camp after all. She wished most desperately that there had been others, for the loss of Malcolm Kerr's jewellery box was also of concern and the messages within it properly interpreted could be damning.

Lord, if only her lady's maid had not packed the letters in her chest under the misguided belief that she should want to take such a treasure with her into her new life. She should have burnt the letters when she had first found them unsent in Ginny's room and tossed away the casement. But there was some jarring immaturity contained in the lines that might one day help her cousin to see that youth had held no chance against the designs of a deceitful and older lover. Nay, no chance at all.

As if her husband could read her mind, he asked the one question she hoped he might not.

'Do you read and write?'

When she nodded, the bleak anger that seemed such a part of him deepened; to fill the growing silence, she carried on the conversation. 'I l-learnt the way of the alphabet in a convent outside York after my p-parents died.'

'There was a note left at the mill. Perhaps later you might show me an example of your hand.'

'L-Later?'

'Tomorrow. I shall not lie with you tonight.'

His words were harsh, thrown off with an easy cadence and with little regard for her feelings.

Nodding, she looked him straight in the eye, rings of grey around blue seen in the bright light of the candles. Something else lingered there, too. Curiosity? Question? She hoped that her smile did not look too forced and that the quiver of desolation on her top lip wasn't noticeable.

Lachlan spent the night alone in his room, dismissing Rebecca when she tried to waylay him, tired of her pouts and sullenness and the way her hair wound around him like serpents in his bed. The train of thought made him frown, for he had been a man who had had many women in his time, seldom finding faults in any, but enjoying what they had to offer. Tonight, however, he only wanted one woman, Grace, with her stutter and her freckles and her fathomless amber eyes. She did not have the artifice of beautiful women. She did not bat her eyes at him or play with her hair like the others were wont to do, the veiled lure of appearance such an easy bait. No, Grace did not have those tricks at all. Her appeal was in her imagination and her secrets and in confessions that had the strange ability to make his heart turn.

He filled a tumbler and held it up against the candlelight, thinking that the gold in the mead was the exact same shade as Grace's eyes in the sunlight, and chastising himself for the very thinking of it. Lord, she had loved his brother and probably still did and had made no secret of the fact that this marriage had been as unwanted on her account as it had been on his.

'Dinna let her get to you, Lach,' he whispered, the fire in

the mill an unsolved mystery and his clan as suspicious of her as they had been of her cousin Stephen when he had come with the news of the death of his brother.

A political alliance to assuage ill feeling between two kings doing their level best to avert war, two kings who would join families who had no wish to unite. Wearied by everything, he finished his drink, pouring himself another to replace the first.

Tonight the cold seeped between the stones of Belridden. He pulled a skin of hide across his shoulders, remembering the moment he had downed this particular stag on the mountains behind the keep two days after his father had died. He had uttered up a prayer then to the soul of a worthy foe, no religion in it either, just the plain knowledge of place and home and hearth. His home. His land. The blood of the stag and the sweat of his brow had mingled in the warmth of breath and the knowledge of life's passing, transient and fragile, the broken dreams of family wrapped in the cord of rope around his father's neck.

A life easily taken.

Malcolm had cut Hugh down, holding the damage to his breast like a mother might a child, his stream of tears contrasting strangely against his own dry cheeks. Lachlan still remembered his attempts at sorrow, paltry endeavours that had sent Malcolm into a fury and widened the growing gap between them, though politics had taken the heart from the Kerrs long before their father had died. It was in the soil of the place, wedged as it was between two kingdoms, a small corridor for the pretensions and greed of men.

The jewelled box on the table caught his attention and

he opened the catch, surprised by the tilt of the green felted lining in the bottom of the bauble, showing askew in the light of the candle. Reaching in, he picked at the layer of card and fabric and when it came away from the silver metal he saw the hidden folded papers in the base.

His wife was nowhere in the castle the next morning. Nowhere in the grounds. Nowhere in the chapel or in the gardens. Anger sharpened until he heard her singing voice echoing strangely across the western wall. He followed the sound, through hedgerows and into a cave he had not known was there.

Grace sat before a shrine of sorts, jars of flowers and a painting of the Holy Family on the wall. Beside her was a series of collected rocks and twigs. When he looked closer he saw one to be of amber, the body of an insect caught within. A moth! To one side of this assortment was the shape of a heart in the dirt, wild clover dotted across it. She stood clumsily as she heard him enter, wiping her eyes with the back of one sleeve.

Grief. For his brother? He had read the notes of love she had written to him, the lines of ardent and flowery prose contained in the jewelled box, and folded in secret, for ever hidden.

When she saw where it was he looked, she kicked at the dirt with her heel, the flower heads scattering.

'How did you find me?'

'I heard you singing and followed the sound.'

'He said no one would hear me here—' She broke off,

guilt in her eyes, and Lach wondered wildly for a second if it was his brother she spoke of?

Silence hung like a shadow between them. The pearls she wore at her throat were double stranded and her hair was plaited with ribbon. Both gown and train were yellow. The colour of anger.

'This is the one place that I do not stutter so b-b-badly. Had you noticed?'

He had not.

'So I should like to tell you that I had n-nothing to do with the burning of your mill. Indeed, my family would attest that I have an aversion to f-fire.'

'I see.' Unexpectedly tears wove the brown in her eyes to gold. He noticed the way the fingers on her right hand turned the ring he had given her. Too big. He would need to remedy that.

'The chapel at Belridden is beautiful, but no one ever uses it. Why?'

'We have no priest here.' A much simpler explanation than the curse Dalbeth had lain on his father in this very room, condemning him for his excesses in women and drink. Every religion had its limits, after all, as to what it was able to condone.

'I am certain if you applied, the church could find—'

He broke into her well-intentioned advice with some of his own.

'You are a newcomer here. It would be far wiser to keep out of things that you know nothing of and leave things as they are, aye.'

'Because the keep is divided and there are some people who could be dangerous to me here?'

Lachlan felt the blood thump in his temples. Who would have told her that? His guess was one of his own soldiers. But why would they jeopardise everything when the safety of David lay fragile enough?

He tried to laugh it off, but saw in his wife's face more than a hint of question.

All of a sudden he was sick of the lies. 'My brother was not, maybe, the man you think he was.'

He looked at the flowers at her feet and she paled dramatically. 'What sort of a man was he, then?'

'A jealous man.'

'Of you?'

He nodded. 'I went with David to France after Edward's victory at Halidon Hill. My brother wished he had been the chosen one and, as he was older than I was, I suppose his reasoning was sound.'

Lord, Lachlan thought to himself, and that was putting a kind face on the reaction. Years of hatred had been difficult to deal with and their father's subsequent death had left Malcolm a punitive and often absent Laird.

Grace felt her heart race. What was he saying of his brother? Could she risk confession here and now and lift the guilt a little from her shoulders? No. She could not chance it, for the bonds of blood ran deep and a wife-by-edict was as nothing against the weight of family. Still, she was fascinated by the cameo of a younger Lachlan Kerr, and whilst he seemed in the way of talking she kept him to it.

'Were you with your king again in England?'

'I was, though the imprisonment there was not a rigorous one. I was able to come back to Scotland on occasion.'

'But your brother was here, still?'

'As Laird it was harder for him to leave.'

The muscles in the side of his jaw tightened as he said it. Not quite the truth, perhaps? She did not dare to question him further as he stood there, a blade in his belt and pale eyes full of secrets. In this cave he looked huge, strong, not a man who had been reared in ease or constraint. He was David's knight, and war was drawn upon his arms and face in the peculiar way that desolation marked those who had known chaos.

Perhaps as marked as her face might become?

Were the ghosts of the badly departed never still? Feeling the rosary in her pocket, she was comforted, tangible history reaching down into the now, reassuring and solid.

'Hail Mary, full of Grace, the Lord is with thee…' The prayer she had recited all her life running in her mind.

She watched as her husband touched the cloth Donald had given her, painted with the image of Jesus. A long welt of redness lay across the top of his left hand. Another injury. She wondered how the wound on his arm had healed, but did not dare to ask him. Today his hair was plaited, the tail of it bound in soft brown leather.

Beautiful. He was beautiful. Every time she saw him anew the harmony of his features combined with sky pale eyes amazed her.

Mine.

For a time.

For the time it took to be ripe with child.

The breath she did not realise she was holding slipped from her body, the secret place between her legs soft-throbbed in want. Would a child be the image of him? She hoped so fervently and her hand, with a will of its own, cradled her stomach. He looked down and his fingers reached out to touch.

Only that, in the cave, with the stream and the gifts of a boy they had helped. Like the Argus moth she was caught in time and space and movement, alive in the warmth of his skin against hers, and hoping, as shards of dust motes swam in the light.

I love you.

Had she said it?

No.

Relief had her reaching out for support against the cold earth in the wall. He would not wish to hear such words from her.

Not yet. Not now. Not ever.

Please, God, make me beautiful. A new prayer in this place of worship. A selfish plea that left her contrite in the face of all the suffering in the world.

'I often talk with God.' Her admission wound a frown into his brow.

'And He answers you?' Irony so easily heard.

She began to shake her head and then changed her mind. 'If you listen hard enough, I like to think that He does.'

The bark of his laughter made her uneasy. 'Such piety and devotion seem ill placed in a woman who responds to the body of a man like yours does.'

Holding her gaze to his, he moved full against her. 'Does the Lord say yea or nay to the joining of a man and a woman in the shrine of this temple, Grace?'

'It is d-d-daytime.'

'And that is your only concern?' Heat narrowed the line of his eyes, bleached in lust.

'I was b-burned once, b-by f-flames.'

'On your thighs?'

She nodded. 'Th-They are ugly in the light.'

In reply he flipped up the yellow wool of her skirt and when she tried to fight him he brought his elbow across the line of her breast and shook his head, fingers searching out the raised skin, scarred by flame, cool in the air of the cave.

When he looked down a single cry of shame escaped her lips and she was still.

Touching. Bending. The quiet run of his tongue against what she had hidden for ever. She lay her head against the wall and closed her eyes. Feeling. Him. Gentle. Her legs widened and his tongue came to the place between. Yellow wool across his shoulders held him as they were joined in the beat of blood and flesh. There were no questions left. Her groans were louder now, calling his name, begging for this thing just beyond her reach and writhing so that his tongue came in further, tight, the musky scent of her body echoing its need. She went over the top of her desire with a sigh and slumped down so that the cold of the floor was against her bottom and she could see his eyes up close.

Not disgust. Not revulsion. Not pity or sympathy. Only a kind of bafflement.

'You like this.' His fingers went to where his mouth had just left.

'And this.' Wetness spilled across her fingers as he brought them to the same place his lay and then drew up the hem of his shirt. 'Your body is calling mine, my *nighean*, like the shout of a bairn as it is released from the warmth it has nae wish to be torn from.'

One deep thrust and he was in, clamping her knees around his own and turning her so that she leaned back and the length of him drove in further. Her cries made him frenzied and he quickened the pace, one hand masking the sound from her lips and the other pulling at the cloth on her bodice.

And this time when the release came the tightening in her body matched his, clenched together in the terrible rush of un-control. Lost. Against time and truth. Only them. Together.

Chapter Eight

He pushed away and left her on the ground, curled in the hazy world of sleep, her skirt ridden up against the scars of fire, revealing the shapely line of one leg.

'Damn it,' he cursed as he strode from the place he had gone to with the intention of telling his wife of the limitations he would like to set on their relationship. He would have her until she fell ripe with the child he required as an heir. That was all.

And instead? He looked back at the entrance to the cave and stopped. If anyone else should find her...

The sun reflected against the trees and he could hear the sweet warbling song of birds, and further off the voices of cottar children playing before supper. All was normal. Just as his life was not. Even now he almost turned back to gather Grace in his arms and take her home. His wife. Her cries as he took her still reverberated in his ears and the subtle smell of flowers still lingered in his nostrils. He could see the red of her hair as it settled against the freckled skin of her throat. Abandoned lust contrasted with her devoutness. His anger had lessened and balanced against what he knew now of her feelings for his brother. The notes had at least told him that.

She had loved him. Every note in that box, signed under the initials of 'GS', had expressed the emotion. Briefly he wondered how they were in her custody given they were sent to his brother. He also wondered why she had not kept the notes that Malcolm must have surely given her in return. Still, they convinced him that his wife was not a murderer and the settling howl of rage and dread deadened a little. At least she was not that!

The arrow that whistled past his temple was hard enough to knock him backwards. Scrambling up and drawing out his dagger, he tried to see just where the missile had come from but, with blood running as a river down into his eyes and colouring his world red, he lost a good moment of searching time. Men ran from the castle gate and from the fields and the mill two hundred yards away.

'What hit ye?' Con's voice, sword out.

Lachlan bent to the fletched arrow reverberating in the trunk of oak and pulled it free, the bodkin-like arrow quivering with the movement. Lord, a head like this could punch easily through even the thickest armour. The ache around his eyes worsened and he closed them for a second before answering.

'Just a graze.' As he said it he noticed Grace behind the men, face flushed and the yellow gown pulled into place. She did not move towards him, but was looking at the wooden tithe barn across the field from their party, and an expression unlike any he had seen paled her face.

Horror and complicity!

Had she seen who had drawn the bow? Could she know him?

The blood pounding in his temple began to drum even harder and, pushing Con with his well-intentioned ministrations to one side, he regathered his wits.

His mind raced at the distance such a weapon could cover. Three hundred or so yards. The barn was well within that parameter.

Drawing out his falchion, he led his men towards the building and away from his wife.

'He's gone,' Lachlan determined some twenty minutes later, kneeling to footprints in the earth that crossed the strip fields of the villagers and then disappeared into thick woodland. The find had confirmed all his fears as the prints were not those of soft brogans or bared feet but of fine shoes. The conclusions from this discovery were written in the anger on his soldiers' faces.

'Who would do this and what would they have to gain from killing ye?'

Lachlan shook his head as the same reasoning turned inside his mind. 'Send retainers into the woods and track where he comes out. That might give us at least some clue. And see if there were others involved.'

The day had darkened, clouds of rain sweeping in from the north and hiding trails, the grey stone walls of his keep wreathed now in mist and shadow. Where was his wife? he wondered. Was this her doing? Was this an easy way to deal with an unwanted husband, the gold coins he had returned to her for her own use enough to set a plan in place? But when could she have done that? She had not been alone since she had come here, save in the cave under the western wall of Belridden.

He said no one would hear me...

He?

Who?

His assailant? Her uncle's man? The fire at the mill and her brooch in the embers. Pieces of a puzzle beginning to add up, slowly.

Grace at the centre of everything!

He hated the way his mind refused to believe it even as his hand tightened about the silk-lined hilt of his sword.

She was waiting for him in her room, sitting on the chair with her hands in her lap, the brown of her eyes dark against the day, and he had to pull his wrath to order before he spoke.

'Did you order this?' His finger touched the wound on his forehead, the blood flow stopped now.

She shook her head.

'But you ken who did. I saw your face, Grace, and you could not hide the fact that you knew him.'

Again she shook her head.

'You lie.'

'I-It was j-just a sh-shadow.' Her fingers turned a kerchief around and around, twisting the cloth in a singular admission of culpability.

'Since you have been at Belridden, we have had as many accidents in days as we have had in years.'

He crossed the room and pulled her up, not carefully either. He saw the fright in her eyes and tempered nothing. 'Who was it, Grace? Who was it you saw?'

'I did not s-see.' He squeezed flesh beneath his fingers as a single tear traced its way across her cheek and dropped on to his hand. He let her go as if he had been stung.

'I dinna believe that you know nothing of it.'

'Then you do n-not know me.'

He went to reply but stopped, something in the glistening of a righteous anger making him waver.

'Perhaps you are right and I dinna know you at all.'

Listening to her husband's retreating footsteps, she stood. She felt numb, sick, confused and, as her hands cradled her face, she tried to make sense of the last few hours.

Malcolm Kerr's servant. She was sure it had been him. The man who would know that his master had not been interested in her at all, but in her young cousin.

Was she going mad? Was the burden of guilt turning her mind into one that saw the face of her foe in a fleeing shadow? She shook her head. Surely it could not be him. Not here. With the knowledge of Ginny's indiscretions he would not remain silent for long within the realm of Belridden, where such revelations would be eagerly listened to.

Placing her fingers against her mouth, she pressed hard

to stop the forming sobs. She could still feel Lachlan's hands upon her body.

One hour and her life had been changed from that to this.

Love.

And lies.

'I love you,' she whispered.

And she did.

When the door opened a few moments later she thought he might have changed his mind and returned. But it wasn't her husband. A woman she had not seen before brought in a pitcher of water and bread, a necklace of dried garlic bulbs worn prominently around her neck.

'For protection against the witchery of a *ban-druidh* if ye are thinking to harm anything else at Belridden,' she explained, her rheumy eyes filled with such hatred that Grace was left breathless with the sheer enmity in them.

She did not see Lachlan the next day or the one after that and finally, when she had had enough of her own company, she bid Lizzie to walk with her to the cave chapel in the late afternoon. She hadn't been down to the Great Hall at all to eat and the only times that she had escaped the confines of her chamber were in the evening when few would see her. Walking today in the sun was wonderful; it had been raining earlier, so there were large puddles on the pathway to the west of the keep. Spreading her arms, she noticed that the ointment she had been religiously using was softening her skin and taking away the dry redness. Even her limp seemed lessened somehow.

They were almost at the mouth of the cave when they heard a strange noise in the bushes. A rustling followed by silence, the green mantle swaying this way and that.

Lizzie jumped back. 'Dinna touch, my Lady, it could be a boar down from the mountains or a sick beast or a…'

A brown nose poked out, the face of its owner following, the eyes of a very large dog looking up at her in supplication.

'He is so ugly.' Lizzie pulled back, but Grace had no thought to merely leave him.

He was frightened and alone, his fur matted with brambles and a long bleeding wound festering on his back leg.

'He is hurt.'

She bent down, their eyes level now. A wary and alert golden glance stared back.

'Do you know this dog, Lizzie? Is he from the keep?'

'In that condition? Nay, he is a stray and should be put down before he harms someone.'

His deep growl made them both jump, but the dog did not move after them. Rather it stopped and waited. Grace got the distinct impression of an animal at the very end of its strength, abandoned and at the mercy of others. There was much in this animal that she felt herself and the want to help it welled.

'Can you return t-to the castle and get a rope, Lizzie?'

'Ye mean to keep it?'

'I mean to h-help it.'

'Ye willna go nearer? If it bites ye and no one is here…'

'I won't touch it, now b-be quick.'

When the maid had gone and the silence again resettled, Grace sat, tucking her skirts between her legs and leaving the material so that she could rise quickly and run if the need arose.

But the animal sat still, very still, neither looking away, nor tending to its wounds, and the dull buzz of flies around the blood was all that could be heard on the air. Even the wind seemed lessened.

'You look like you need some love,' she said finally and his ears pricked against the sound. There was a considerable notch out of one of them and the other did not quite stand straight. 'I could help you if you w-would let me?' Her fingers reached out and he did not pull away. Encouraged, she lent further forwards and when her fingers touched his fur, he only turned his head slightly.

He didn't have the softness of a pet, but the pelt of a dog who had been through some hard times. She smiled as he butted his nose against the heel of her hand before stiffening, the hackles of his fur rising proud along the skeletal ridge of his spine.

Startled, Grace scrambled up. Lachlan stood there, and the growl of the animal echoed threateningly.

Suddenly she knew just exactly who this dog reminded her of.

'I instructed you not to leave the castle without a guard.'

'I could n-not find one of your s-soldiers and Lizzie was w-with me.'

The frown on his forehead deepened, but he did not pursue the argument, instead looking down at the dog.

'I f-found him in the bushes. He's w-wounded.'

'A leg-hold trap by the looks.' Putting out his hand, he

moved forwards. 'Animals who are wounded can be unpredictable.' Grace saw how he shielded her with his body. As unpredictable as he was!

She watched as he slipped the rope around the dog's neck, the line of his fingers checking for other injuries.

'He's some sort of a bloodhound and probably a hunter. Not a pure breed though, for you can see that in the shape of his ears.'

'You know about d-dogs,' she queried, 'yet you do n-not have any yourself?'

'I travel a lot.' The animal licked his face as he knelt.

Travelled, but never settled. She saw how the mark of the arrow on his forehead had faded into a light red line, making him look even more menacing and reckless than he usually did.

'Could his wounds be m-mended?'

'Probably, but that's not the question, is it, Grace?'

'It's not?' She always felt like this with Lachlan Kerr. Out of kilter and on guard.

'Nay. More is the question as to why you should want me to?'

'I d-don't understand.'

'When David first mentioned your name as a wife, I thought of my brother and his penchant for the type of women I had no interest in, and I wondered. But then you came and you were different.'

'Not as p-pretty?'

He shook his head and her heart sank. 'Not that. Different as in…honest, direct, truthful.'

Now she knew where he was heading.

'And I thought to myself, Lachlan, you have been years and years in the company of those who would say one thing and do another, for politics you understand, and after the Bruce there were many enemies.'

'Of David?'

'And Scotland! But now I am not so certain that you are that much different at all.' His finger traced the mark of the arrow. 'Who was it, Grace? Who did this to me?'

Lachlan or Ginny? Did she risk answering and hope to find in him a man who would be sworn to silence? How long would it be after all before Kenneth MacIndoe spilled the truth?

Before she could answer he began to speak again.

'My guess is that it was someone who you know behind the tithe barn in the shadows and then I would ask why is it that you will not say it?'

Her rising blush made him continue.

'Are you a murderer, Grace? Is that what you would hide?'

'No.'

'Then do you shelter one? Your cousin Stephen, perhaps, or your uncle? They were as scared of me as you are, aye.'

The paleness of his eyes seemed to bore right through her, though when she said nothing he began to pull the dog towards him, softly at first, and then with more pressure. She was surprised when the dog acquiesced, sidling up to his legs in the way of one who was a favoured pet. 'Dogs represent a home, you see. A settled home where people stay and stay. We dinna have that with these lies between us, so I am wondering, if you should give your heart to such a one, where it would take you?'

Her heart!

She looked up sharply, confused by the dreadful certainty that perhaps it was not the dog he spoke of after all. But he gave nothing away, this lord of lands that were threatened by everyone and she saw how he must have looked in the court of London where he had gone to negotiate the release of a monarch whom Edward had no interest in letting go.

Persuasion, diplomacy and intellect. Nay, it was not just in war and battle that Lachlan Kerr excelled.

And yet in the asking of his question she had detected something that she had not imagined to find there. Longing for a home.

'How did your parents die?' Perhaps if she knew something of his family.

'Badly.' He looked away as Lizzie came down the track towards them with two youths.

'It took me a time to find them, Laird,' she puffed, and Grace saw that they were armed.

'You w-would not kill him?'

Icy pale eyes bored into her before he turned and led the small group out of the woods.

She decided to call the black dog Dexter, after her grandfather, for he deserved a name that was strong, as strong as he was to have withstood the wildness of this part of the country and the marks of the trap still evident in the fur on his leg.

Another secret blossomed within her.

It was past thirty days since she had last had her menses, her breasts full and aching, and the very thought of it made her feel…whole.

A mother.

Her.

She had given up hoping that it would ever be so after her sixteenth birthday when no man had so much as looked at her, and so the wonder of it now made everything possible.

He held her in his arms and whispered the words as his fingers crossed the full stretch of stomach. My child. My wife. I will love you both for ever and ever.

Grace pondered on the meanings of her daydreams. At Grantley she had had such visions daily. Here, they were fewer and further between and she could not imagine Lachlan Kerr saying anything like those words in reality. This was another change in her. Before she had believed such fantasies as almost real. Now she knew better; the lovemaking in her imagination was nowhere near as wonderful as that outside of it.

There had been no word at all on Kenneth MacIndoe. It was as though he had disappeared back into the place he had come from and Lachlan had not mentioned the incident again. For that at least she was glad, as some sort of truce settled between them, a suspension of anger, a fragile resurrection of peace, and, although he avoided her bed and this guarded carefulness was tiring, anything was better than anger.

Today they had visitors at the keep. A friend of Lachlan's had arrived from Edinburgh and she had been asked down to join the men for dinner.

The dress she wore was of the darkest blue, almost midnight, and a silver hooped belt sat across the line of her hips. She had left her hair down after washing it in the early morning and her curls were soft with the special soap Lizzie had concocted for the task. Dexter sat by her bed watching, his golden eyes waiting for her to move towards the door so that he in turn could follow, and Grace smiled at his alertness and at his loyalty.

When she entered the hall Lachlan stood and the man next to him did the same.

'John Murray, Lord of Bothwell and Avoch, I would like to introduce you to my wife, Lady Grace.'

Murray's hand was warm when she took it and so was his smile. Lachlan on the other hand looked tired, and there was a new bruise on the line of his cheek. His glance did not quite meet her own as he helped her into her seat, his manners tonight those of the court, his hand staying on the small of her back. A show for the benefit of his friend, perhaps?

'I have heard much about you, Lady Grace.'

The sentiment seemed genuine enough though she wondered at his sources. 'I hope it was not f-from the court j-jesters, my Lord?'

He laughed. 'Your husband could barely wait to return to Belridden last time I saw him and now I can well see why.'

For a second her bravado faltered. She was unused to such compliments and even a man as obviously kind as John Murray would have his reasons for lying. Still, her courage was bolstered remarkably as Lachlan poured her a drink, his eyes wandering to the swell of flesh above the neckline of her gown with a glitter of lust and need. Grace breathed in deeply so that the bounty of her breasts would seem larger.

'John is on his way to the court of London, Grace.' Upending his glass, he helped himself to another.

'One of the reasons for my visit here is that David asked me to see how you two fared. I hope I can tell him that his meddling in the affairs of the heart was a resounding success?'

'You can see that it is such.' Carefully Lachlan moved, so that his arm lay against her forearm. Feeling the warmth, Grace longed to simply lay her fingers across his and hold on, but didn't. This was his charade and she wanted to see just how far he would take it.

Behind them the servants lingered, refilling glasses and restocking plates of food. A flush of want stained her cheeks and she looked down, trying to take stock, trying to be this woman who was a wife and loved, even for a moment in front of this guest from Edinburgh.

'David was hopeful for news of a Kerr heir. With Margaret murdered and Joan sickly, he has need of his nobles' progeny for the future stability of the Borderlands, Lach.'

'And when there is some news he will be the first to be told it.' Her husband's voice was cool, the queries as to his personal circumstances unwelcome, even from a friend, to a private man who gave little away!

'Without a Bruce son there is mounting opposition in Parliament.'

'Then isolate those who would oppose David. Pick the

king's enemies off one at a time and hold them to the royal mercy.'

'Come back to Edinburgh then, Lachlan, and help us do it.'

'Nay. I have served David well for nearly all the years of my life and Belridden's promise of peace grows on me. Besides, Scotland has a need for strength here in the Eastern Marches.'

'What of the Tournaments? Would ye come for those at least?'

'I never have.'

John laughed. 'So Belridden is home? Then I hope God smiles on ye kindly and there will be the promise of many canty bairns.'

He lifted his tumbler and Grace perceived in his glance, just for a moment, the same look she so often saw in her husband's.

Loss!

The true cost of being David's minion was not measured in lands or gold, but in the deprivation and forfeiture of home and hearth. She wondered where Murray's family was as she raised her glass and gave him a toast.

'To y-your quick r-return to Scotland and I hope you will c-come to stay on the way b-back.'

'I would be delighted to, Lady Kerr. *Slainte mhath.*'

'To your good health,' Lachlan translated, and in his words she heard a flat undercurrent that made her wary.

God, Lachlan thought as he looked on, the lies and deceit thick in the air around him and the strong ale making him light-headed. Light-headed enough to say something he might regret later about politicking and the creed of a king who could believe in the possibility of an English succession? Scotland would go to pieces and the world would be damned! He wondered for a frantic second what his whole life's work had actually been for, and the arrow in his chest at Neville's Cross which had almost killed him. Twelve thousand men against eight until Dunbar and Steward had turned away, leaving their ranks exposed. He hated such cowardice with the passion of one who would always despise traitors and yet David was shifting away from Scottish independence at an alarming speed.

Nothing seemed right any more!

Nothing save for Grace if he could just cast aside his doubts about her.

Just for this time he wanted to believe in something and someone. His fingers tightened and he was pleased when she did not pull away as he listened to her speak to John. She was a lady who had been brought up with the ability to keep a conversation going despite the stammer. He also noticed how she made it a point to thank his servants for any help given.

He wished he had not read her love notes in Malcolm's jewellery box spilling out heart and hopes. She had never said anything like that to him, not once, and he knew that she had seen exactly who it was behind the tithe barn after the arrow had almost killed him.

Compromised. Again.

John was laughing at Grace's retelling of her finding the dog in the bushes earlier that afternoon. She seemed to be calling him Dexter; the right-hand field of a shield perhaps, or some family name, he knew not which. But the hound hung below her chair, his yellow eyes drowning in every move she made, watching, hopeful. He wondered fleetingly if his own eyes mirrored the same emotions. That need for people around him he could trust and depend on amongst the vagaries of policy-making and greed.

Anger lacerated longing as he drank the last of the ale and he could see on John's and Grace's faces a question as to his silence. But he couldn't help it. Not tonight. Not with the promise of everything he could never have, so damn bloody near.

'You'll keep the dog then, Lach?'

'I cannot see Grace being able to part with him—besides, his leg is not yet mended.'

His wife turned at that and gave him a smile that made him want to vouch her any other pet she might wish for, but the servants brought out the dessert and all the room's attention focused on the platter.

Save his. At the back of the hall a small group of soldiers congregated. Rebecca stood with them and Lizzie, Grace's maid. Something about the way they watched his wife made him uneasy and his hand went to the hilt of his sword with a mind of its own. Then they dispersed and the moment was gone. He almost wondered if he had imagined the incident or had given the episode a malevolence that it was lacking. Still, he swore himself to caution and decided he would instruct Grace on the morrow on at least the rudiments of self-defence.

Chapter Nine

Lachlan took her walking far from the keep and Grace wondered as to his intent. His belt was threaded with a half a dozen daggers and his hair today was pulled back in a tight knot. He did not wait as he strode through the under-growth, did not hold back the wayward branches or even turn to check that she still walked behind him. No, today he was focused on some inside thing and her presence barely registered.

Finally he stopped. They stood in a glade of sorts, the trees tall around them and canopied across an afternoon sky.

With care he took a blade from his belt before opening her palm and placing the weapon on it.

'Belridden is a keep that is divided and if you should be caught in the middle of a *stramash*, then there are things that you should know in your defence. Have you ever before held a knife against an enemy, Grace?'

She could only shake her head and watch as he closed her fingers around the leather hilt of the weapon.

'Feel the weight of it and imagine where the true balance

of protection lies.' He jiggled the steel this way and that and bid her close her eyes. Blinded, she focused on what he asked.

After a moment the shape lay equally poised on her palm, gentle almost with the breeze off the stream beside them and the spongy moss under her feet.

'It feels…still.' No other words for it. She was pleased that she did not stutter here in the silence.

'Good.' His finger laid against the base of her right thumb. 'Now remember that stillness as you open your eyes, for the heft of a blade lies mostly in the weight of thrust and counter-thrust.' He was beside her, close, the breath of his words on her cheek and the tips of his fingers turning the knife into the space between forefinger and thumb. Hard hooked, the handle sat still, the leather covering unfamiliar as her grasp closed around it.

He checked the angle and nodded. 'A dagger like this is best used up close and with the most surprise that you can muster for an attack. They will not expect resistance from you.'

'They…?' She let her query tail off.

'Anyone is suspect. Remember that. Anyone.'

'Not your friend, John?'

'No, Grace, not him.'

'Or Connor?'

This time he shook his head. 'My brother ruled the keep for years and some of his supporters still reside in the castle, waiting for me to make a mistake.'

'Like marrying me?'

He laughed. 'If it were just that simple, I should not be out here teaching you the art of killing a man. Nay, I should be enjoying your wares in the comfort of my own bed and behind the safety of a heavy lock.'

'They want you dead.' Suddenly she understood. 'And me with you?'

'There are whispers circulating that Malcolm may still be alive and that an heir between us may not be to their liking.'

A rush of blood covered her face. She had told him nothing of her lack of menses and was pleased to see that his face was blank of any knowledge of it. Just an innocent question, then? But the rumours about his brother…

'Do you think these rumours could be true?'

'You tell me, Grace. The gully was deep and Stephen said that you had it well searched, but with the river at the bottom it could be possible.'

Dread made her pale.

'And those who support Malcolm are not David's advocates, are they?'

'Nay, and that is why I am here. The Marches are the buffer between two kingdoms who have been at war for as long as any of us can remember. If Steward or Douglas should lay their hands upon the south and take hold…'

'War would follow. So John Murray did not only visit to see that the alliance we have formed was tenable, did he?'

'No, which is why you must learn to defend yourself.' He stepped back before extracting his own blade. Grace saw instantly how easily it fitted into his fist.

Please God let Malcolm be dead. The refrain was like a chant in her body.

'If I came at you like this, what would you do?'

She raised the knife.

'Nay. From below. You will have more strength that way. And come in hard. Like this.'

The sound was of air, and the quickness of movement barely seen.

She copied and he smiled.

'You are a good mimic. If you practise that while I watch, you will get the true way of it.'

Thrust and step back. Thrust and step back. In a few moments she was as tired as she could ever remember.

'Is fighting always this hard?'

'You have not connected with anything yet.' He unwrapped his standard and laid it around the bough of a tree. 'Make for the chevron,' he instructed.

When she did so the whole knife jarred against her wrist and she gave a yelp of pain, dropping the knife and holding the sting of her hand.

'Bone is as hard, Grace,' he said as he took her fingers between her own, rubbing back the warmth and feeling. 'But if you don't know these things, then death is harder, aye.'

The strange rings on his wrists were easy to see as his shirt fell back. 'How did this happen?' Her first finger came out to touch the lines of black, and stillness came upon him.

'Vanity. Ancient Catholics viewed tattooing as a sign of maturity. Did you know that?'

'No.'

'I was told so once by a man whom I thought I had much to learn from and over a fire at Vironfosse he drew in the design and filled it with ashes. I was almost fourteen so the thought of such an encryption was powerful.'

Three strands formed a complex braid, weaving across each other, a scar dissecting the band above his thumb.

'And this?' She touched the raised welt.

He shrugged. 'David had many enemies that became mine as well.'

'Even now?'

He nodded and the world around them fell still, no birdsong or river running, no wind through the trees or insects around the last flowers before the winter.

There was only a smile as his lips came down across her own, and again when he undid the ties of her kirtle, her nipples hardening in the breeze, the paleness of her skin startling as his hands followed the shape of her shoulders and breasts and waist.

'It seems that I cannae stay away from you, *mo nighean,* even though I would will it.' He took a breath and confessed further. 'Your body is as a home to me and I have nae had many.'

The bright chevron banner on the bough unfurled in the wind and floated to the ground beside them. In invitation she was to think later; to a bed in the glade of trees, and the whole world far from here. No enemies or politics. She saw how he hesitated, as though fighting a battle to leave.

When his breath shook, she knew that she had won and pulled him down beside her on the silk of his family standard. He was a man raised in Europe, so both heraldry and plaid were of equal importance. A complex man, the true pull of Scotland watered down by other teachings. She imagined him with Philip in the French court and again in Edward's palaces, treading lightly lest those of other persuasions should harm his king.

He was loyal to the idea of a Scotland no longer under the lordship of the English, starting here in the Borderlands, the first bastion against the disinherited Barons of Balliol and the pretensions of Robert Stewart.

In harm's way! Of a sudden she knew that war would come to these lands and soon. The shiver of dread made her skin pucker.

'You are cold?' He loosened his belt and wrapped the generous standard around them. Cocooned in red and green, the light from the day threw strange hues upon their skin.

Like bruises.

Sometimes she hated her imagination. She pushed the fear away and concentrated on now. Just now.

'I have been away from this land for so verra long… Sometimes I wish—' He stopped and she waited.

'Sometimes I wish that I had not.'

Simple, and said like a confession that was for her ears only. It was a gift given in confidence and honesty and, with the battle marks of many years drawn upon him, it was a rare gift indeed. Her hand pulled at the hem of his shirt and she found the burning force of all that was held between them, isolation quashed in the single act of connection.

'You are b-beautiful.' *Far more beautiful than me,* she almost added, but the words would not quite come.

She looked into his eyes, there, six inches from her own,

in the light, with their breaths mingling, looked into the depth of paleness and saw desire. For her.

Powerful and true. Passion felt through a blinded touch. Moving inwards to each other. The centre shifted. No longer just each other.

Let me touch and forget the world around us. When she groaned it was not in pain but in wonder and the rolling shards of oneness that pinned them to each other were elemental and complete.

They did not speak afterwards, each locked in a silence that was their own, a thin and tenuous bond against the secrets that would divide them.

Grace closed her eyes and breathed in the smell of him, the beauty of his body and the wild thumping of his heart.

He moved.

Again.

She closed her eyes and let him do as he willed, the thought crossing her mind that it was more than war and politics after all that he had been taught in the days of his training in France.

Much, much more.

Hours later they walked back to the castle, the instruction of defence forgotten under an onslaught of something entirely different.

It was dark, and the moon illuminated both footfall and path. They did not touch, did not accidentally fall into the sphere of the other. There was too much at stake and too little to stop what it was that they now both feared; that wordless thing that held couples to ransom even as it held the world at bay.

Not yet for them. Not yet.

When the guards hailed from the ramparts and put down the bridge, they crossed quickly and left each other.

In her room Grace looked at her reflection in the mirror and was surprised to see that she had not altered, had not changed, had not become what she could feel inside, where a breathless and burning want singed every fibre of her body.

She smiled and the woman who smiled back looked… almost pretty. Amazement rose and she laid a finger along the line of her cheek as Lachlan had done, careful, arousing, even the memory of it evoking an excitement she could barely fathom.

I love you.

She wanted to say it, wanted to shout it, the bare echo of the words all that she could feel. She wished that her cousins were here, to tell, to ask, to query as to the validity of her discovery and his response, to see through their women's eyes just exactly what was real.

Perhaps none of it was.

Perhaps lust was all that he felt and she was an easy target with her unconditional giving. Again and again.

A scratching at her door made her stop and turn, though before she had even opened it she knew who it was.

Dexter.

The feel of him against her was comforting and warm, his lolling wet tongue making her laugh out loud.

I love you, I love you, I love you.

Guileless and adoring, no matter what.

Lachlan pulled off his shirt and waded into the lake, the moon as distinct as he had ever seen it. Tonight he did not dive. Tonight he stood there with the blackness lapping around his chest and the infinity of the heavens above him, his eyes scouring the far-off bank and tracing the line of land from water to mountain. Kerr land as far as he could see. His land. Not just his father's, but his grandfather's and the grandfather before that one. Good men, honourable men, they were trustees of a past that went beyond time, beyond memory.

One day his own sons would stand here in this very spot and be reminded of the ancestors that lay in this earth of toil and blood, ancestors who would reach with quiet hands down into the moment and reassure, like they were doing now to him.

Malcolm. Hugh.

For this once he did not hate them, and the relief was immense.

Grace was his. His, despite the notes and her admissions of love in his brother's jewelled box. No one could have lain in that chevron silk and come out unchanged. He lifted his fingers to his mouth, trying to taste the last of her, but she was gone. The water around his manhood played with him just as she had. A little memory.

'God, help me,' he found himself saying and this time in the foreverness of the sky above and the water below, he found that he meant it.

'God, please, please help me.' There was a shifting in his soul. Belief was still there after all the bleakness of what had been. He smiled at the thought and then smiled again as a shooting star crossed the heavens, its tail of light reflected in the water.

A sign from above?

He made a cross over his heart.

'Pater noster, qui es in caelis, sanctificetur nomen tuum…'

Our Father, Who art in Heaven, Hallowed be Thy name…

Chapter Ten

Rebecca McInness sought her out the next morning. She had been crying. Grace could see it in the swollen redness of her face. For once she did not look beautiful and she hoped that Lachlan Kerr might have seen her this way, a thought that she recanted when the woman handed her flowers picked from the path by the caves on the western side of Belridden.

Eleanor Kerr, who usually kept to her rooms, lurked behind, her dark eyes flinting when Grace made the mistake of including Lachlan's grandmother in her smile.

Carefully she looked away and concentrated on what the younger woman was saying.

'It has come to my notice that I may have hurt ye in my actions and I would like to apologise.'

Rebecca's carefully concocted sorrow sounded as though it came from nowhere near her heart.

Still, Grace took the flowers and inclined her head. 'Thank you.' She could not quite work out what else to say.

'Eleanor feels it may be best for me to leave Belridden and go to stay with my mother's people.'

This was said with a great deal of supplication and as if she would wish Grace to say different out here before the dowager of this castle and with all the servants listening.

'I th-think perhaps that E-Eleanor is right.'

For the first time the older woman's eyes met hers without criticism even as the tears ran down the alabaster cheeks of Lachlan's mistress. Grace, however, had no time to ponder her reaction, for voices outside caught their attention.

Her husband stepped through the doorway and Grace could tell that he had been training his soldiers, for straps of leather were still tied about his wrists and two swords lay in scabbards at his belt. Connor and Ian both flanked him and were laughing about something he had said, though their amusement vanished as Rebecca ran to the Laird in a flood of tears. His glance went to Grace, brows raised in question, but he made no move to interfere and the girl, seeing that he meant to just let her go, began crying louder as she made for the stairs.

Dexter broke the awkwardness with his rush at the men, tail wagging furiously and his big lolling tongue licking Lachlan's shoes.

Grace noticed how her husband's hand crept to the ears of the dog, scratching and petting, as he accepted a mug of water given to him by one of the servants.

With his laughter and the dog's love and the sunbeams slanting in through the arched windows of the Great Hall, she thought that he looked…happy, or at least much less bleak than the man she had married or the man who had sat at dinner last night and barely spoken.

Eleanor was also happier this morning as she walked across to sit at a table with her grandson.

'Perhaps we might have an outing to the river bend tomorrow, Lachlan, the last one of the season with the clan children and their parents? We have need of some good times at Belridden to keep us content for the winter.'

As Lachlan nodded, Grace saw how the servants behind him smiled, and knew too that the word of such an occasion would be around the castle before very long. A simple enjoyment. She found herself looking forward to the day with an unprecedented excitement.

Lachlan finished writing out the day's accounts and went to find his wife. Her room was empty when he reached it though, and he sent a servant to find her, reasoning that she might still be in the Great Hall planning the morrow's outing with his grandmother. Hoping that she would come soon, he crossed the room and picked up her brush, the red of her hair entwined in the bristles. When he put it down he saw that the insect caught in amber was placed near it.

Grace kept a careful hold on her treasures and the thought made him wonder if she had been given many. Remembering he still had not shown her the clip he had bought from Edinburgh, he dug it out of his sporran. It seemed fitting that tonight she should be given something to celebrate…what? He did not know and shook his head wryly.

Finally there was a noise of steps down the passage and then there she was. Dexter was right behind her.

'I am sorry that y-you had to wait. E-Eleanor was very

keen to discuss all the details. She kept f-forgetting even after I had told her.'

'Just as long as ye dinna tell her that she is forgetting things.'

Unexpectedly she laughed and the sound was joyful and true.

'When you smile you look almost beautiful.'

'Almost?' Said teasingly as if she would want more.

'Verra, then. Verra beautiful.'

'With an empty bed beside you and an empty night before you, I might c-consider your sentiments questionable.'

Reaching into his pocket, he brought out the clip. 'Perhaps then a gift might melt your hardened heart?'

'For me?' All humour fled as her teeth worried her upper lip in uncertainty.

'I got it weeks ago. You should have had it before now.'

'But I have nothing to give you in r-return.'

'Do you not, Grace?' The thread of lust made his meaning easily decipherable as he walked forwards and laid it in her hands. 'The merchant said that it was from the holy city of Constantinople.'

Her fingers closed on the present. In the light the embellished figurine of a knight on his horse was easily seen.

'Did you wear s-such armour?' she asked as her finger skimmed across breastplate and pauldron.

'In France I did.'

'But not here?'

He shook his head. 'I haven't taken part in the tournaments.'

'Because…?'

'I lost friends in the battles against the English so I could never see the point of countrymen losing their lives to each other under the banner of entertainment. Besides, the rules of entry were always stringent.'

'The art of chivalry was not your inclination, then?' She looked down at the clip in her hand and smiled. 'I could argue differently and my uncle was of the opinion that you would do very well for me.'

'What sort of a man is your uncle?'

Business again. Grace was almost getting used to the way his focus would shift from one thing to another so quickly.

'A good man.'

'One of Edward Balliol's men?'

'A very l-long t-time ago.'

'Like your own father was?'

The world began to spin for Grace, around and around; feeling the bed behind her, she sat down.

Yes. Yes. Yes. The blood on her mother's dress had exactly matched the colour of her shoes.

'You h-have been asking questions about m-me?'

'About your family, Grace. About your parents. About their deaths outside York. Some would say that your father paid dearly for his tinkering in the politics of a country he had little reason to like.'

She could only nod and listen as he continued.

'The lands of your grandfather had stretched along the Western Marches and were lost when Robert Stewart signed the Treaty of Edinburgh. And so I ask again, Grace, what sort of a man is your uncle?'

'One who is different from my f-father. One who would not jeopardise his family for the g-gain of gold.'

She saw the muscles along the side of his jaw tighten.

Fire stinging her legs. Mama. Strange and dangerous men calling her name and the earth against her cheeks. Damp. Cold. Dark. Whispers. Her father's fault. The end of childhood.

'What did she look like? Your mother?'

'She w-was beautiful.'

The softness in his eyes kept her silent.

'I heard it said in Edinburgh that you only began to stutter after the incident and that you were in the woods for a good two days before they found you curled up under the trunk of an oak.'

'I l-loved her.'

'And him? Did you love your father, too?

'Yes.' The word was forced from her, forced from anger and desolation and regret. Forced from what she had lost and what she was now left with.

Blame juxtaposed against loyalty.

'Good men can make mistakes as easily as bad ones, Grace,' he said as one who knew. Her face turned to his.

'My m-mother had not wanted to go to Y-York. He made us go.'

The hollow ache in her throat was building by the moment, fault and guilt mixed with the memory of sitting on her father's knee whilst he told her stories. He was not all bad then, his fingers brushing against the red in her hair, the light in his exactly the same shade as her own.

Trembling, she tried in that echo of goodness to find a pathway out of such an all-consuming grief. To survive!

'My father called to me as he was dying, before the others came. He told me he had not meant to involve us in his politics and that he was sorry. I had forgotten he even said it until now.' Her fingers slid across the shiny shell of the clip she held still, tracing the outlines of an etched knight. Seeing words set inside, she held it up to the light.

Miserere nobis. ' "Have mercy." Did you kn-know this was here?'

He shook his head. 'Perhaps the Christian Byzantine empire has provided you with an answer for your faith?'

'In God?'

He shook his head. 'In yourself.'

Suddenly she did laugh. 'This from a man who b-believes in nothing?'

'Did believe in nothing,' he answered obliquely and pulled her up against his strength and certainty. Her long-trapped anger began to dissolve, change and reform into sorrow, for choices badly made and for the last uttered pleas of forgiveness from a father who had taken a wrong turn and still loved her.

Perhaps Lachlan was right after all.

Perhaps good men could make mistakes as easily as bad ones. She leant into him and he held her as the moon rose in the eastern sky, drawing light across darkness, the passage of minutes measured only by warmth.

* * *

She woke at dawn, suddenly, the sound of birds outside and calling. Lachlan lay beside her, but she did not move because she knew how easily he was roused even at the slightest of noises.

Asleep he looked less austere, softer, the length of his dark lashes against his cheeks surprising, like an angel, a battered angel whose beauty made all those who looked on him wonder.

They had held hands last night and talked, not the talk of lovers but that of friends. Talked of childhood memories and favourite places and times in their lives where happiness had lingered. Still their fingers were joined, fallen into the softness of sleep and trust, holding on to the promise of unity that shivered between them.

Beguiling.

Addictive.

Safe.

She smiled and looked up into a pale gaze that did not waver.

'Good morning.' He raised up their still-clasped hands. 'I have nae slept with a woman like this before.'

'In friendship?'

'Nay,' he returned before rolling over on top of her, pinning her against the softness of the bed. 'In much more than that, aye.'

Chapter Eleven

Grace lay back on the blanket set in a sheltered glade and looked up at the sky.

'Scotland is so b-beautiful. So much w-wilder than Grantley.' Lachlan's grandmother beside her smiled.

'*Oui*, that it is and a good thing, too, for the world and its problems to be distant.'

She could not disagree, not today with the warmth unexpected, Dexter at her side and the promise of a cold winter just around the corner. Turning to the river, she saw Donald with a stick in his hand heading for the stream, his mother Mary sitting behind with a group of younger children and a baby at her breast.

Grace's eyes went to that child, tiny and helpless. She wondered how it must feel to hold such a one, to feed it and love it and care for it. Her menses still had not arrived.

'When I had Lachlan's father I was fourteen years old.'

Grace glanced quickly around at Eleanor. She must have seen where she had been looking.

'Hugh was a twin, you know. His sister died at birth

and I often think about her when I see little ones like Mary's babe.'

'My husband and his f-father did not seem close…'

'My son was a selfish boy and then a selfish man, but the light went out of his world when his wife died.'

'How old was Lachlan w-when that happened?'

'Almost six. Just before he went with David to France.' Her expression told Grace that she had not been pleased with the arrangement and she was just about to ask her further about it when a small face peeked out from the woods on the other side of the bank, the plaid he wore different from that of the Kerrs. She watched as Donald lifted his hand and waved and then the stranger was gone, swallowed up by the thick greenery.

The six or so soldiers who had come with them to the river bend did not seem perturbed and so she relaxed, hoping that Lachlan would come to join them soon, for he had been detained by the man overseeing the rebuilding of the water wheel.

Excited voices caught her attention. Donald now lay against the bough of a tree over the water, catching large flat leaves that floated down in the current. A younger boy watched him, giving instructions as to when the next leaf would leave the clumped mass caught in an eddy. Grace remembered playing such games with her cousins when she had been young, but the crack of a breaking branch banished daydreams, and she watched as Donald simply slid off the tree and into the deep water beneath him.

Mary ran as fast as she did and Dexter was on her heels,

but before they had reached the river another body shot out from the bushes on the other side of the embankment and leapt into the water, making straight for Donald.

It was the boy who had watched them from the forest. The soldiers who accompanied them also ran nearer, but they were not near enough. Already Grace could see Donald going under again, getting weaker, white fingers grasping at nothingness.

Undoing the ties on her dress she stepped out of it, the shift beneath at least allowing her movement that the heavier cloth would not. Her boots followed.

'What are ye doing?' Eleanor held her back.

'I can swim. My father taught me to swim,' she shouted, throwing off her grasp and running, ordering the dog to stay as it, too, tried to enter the water.

The cold hit her as an ache taking away breath, the blackness of a Scottish river much different from the clear streams of her girlhood. But she kept wading towards Donald, ten yards, five now, the boy's hands grasping her own from beneath the surface, clinging, pulling down.

She had not reckoned on the strength of his desperation or the pull of the current and as her legs were dragged out from underneath, Donald's thrashing feet landed hard against hers beneath the water. Breath left her and she felt her lungs exploding as she went under, the child's hair standing up on his head and wild eyes wide through the bubbled greenness.

When they came up again white water enveloped them, the shouts from those still on the bank and Dexter's barks dulled by the liquid in her ears. The other boy was there too, helping, his small face etched in frowns.

'Can you hold that arm?' she panted, grateful when he nodded as she pulled on the other one. In towards the bank they swam, slowly, the current on this side as strong as she had felt in any water. The mud was beneath her feet and then gone again, deeper green. Bottomless.

The branch hit them both, unexpectedly swirling in the eddy of a side channel, and then the older child was gone, knocked away by the sheer force of it all.

Hands reached for Donald, though. Soldiers' hands, strong hands. Safety.

A choice now?

Save one or save them both?

She simply let the warmth go and fell backwards, floating with the current downstream, voices further away and lost in silence. Then it was just her!

He was lying in the water face down when she got to him and she kicked for the side. More debris hit them, a smaller branch cracked against her upper arm and another against her shin. Tears smarted with the pain, but she refused to panic. Not now when they were so close. Twenty yards, and then ten, and finally the mud beneath her feet, thick and deep, but solid.

Turning him over when she had gained a good footage, she beat his chest as she had seen her father do once to the body of a man who did not breathe.

His coughing reassured her and she sat on the bank hacking, trying to take the air she needed and thankful to be alive. Finally they were able to speak, both their voices croaky with the amount of water they had swallowed.

'You…saved…me?'

'Who are y-you?'

'Callum Elliot. I am the…eldest son of…the Laird of the Elliots.'

Lord! Grace almost laughed. Elliot was the man who had insulted her in the forest, and from a clan with no love lost for the Kerrs.

Blood ran across his left cheek from a deep cut where the log had glanced off him and his hair fell across it, picking up the colour, sun-bleached tingeing pink.

'If you had not b-been there, I might not have b-been able to save Donald.' She needed to give him back his confidence.

He looked up at that, the blue in his eyes the exact same colour as a midnight sky. 'The boy? His name is Donald? I have seen him before in the woods between our keeps.'

'He is about y-your age and an adventurer as well, so it is little wonder you two should have crossed paths. I am Grace, by the way.'

Despite the shift she wore being almost see-through and the absurdity of the situation, he held out his hand, and she took it.

Already they could hear calling from a distance, the sound of soldiers and then Dexter. For a second she thought she heard Lachlan's voice, deeper than the others and closer.

'I cannae let them find me here. If my father ever knew…' He stood up and sat down again just as quickly.

'I don't think that you h-have a choice, Callum,' she answered softly and laid her arm around his shoulder as she called back.

Lachlan slashed through the trees like a man possessed, though when he saw her he stopped and took breath, the fierce anger on his brow replaced by a different sort of fury. Dexter had no such qualms, his big tongue lolling across both her face and Callum's.

'For a woman who is frightened of her own shadow, you seem surprisingly good at risking your life to save others.'

'When did you c-come?'

'Just in time to see you let go of my soldier's hands and float off down the river.'

'Callum is hurt.'

'Callum?'

'The Laird of Elliot's s-son.'

'Gods!'

Not the reply she might have expected. She felt the child tense at her side.

'The Laird of the Kerrs will not h-hurt you, Callum. You do not have to w-worry at all.'

Her voice carried and she thought she saw her husband smile as he came forwards, stripping off his Highland sark and placing it across her head. His plaid was the only thing shielding his nakedness.

'My soldiers are right behind,' he explained; the bulging strength of his muscles in the afternoon sun was breathtaking. The linen fell across her skin as a sheath, warm and dry. She coughed as he brought her to him, roughly, the line of his finger tracing that of her jaw.

'You will have a bruise here,' he said, 'and here,' he added, the mark on her neck sore as she pulled away.

Still he did not let her go far, his hand resting on the line of her bottom, the water from her shift marking his plaid with darkness.

Mary and Eleanor crowded around Callum, giving him praise for his bravery and offering a blanket. Grace was pleased that they did so, because reaction to everything had suddenly set in and she found herself shaking as uncontrollably as he did.

'I—I d-don't k-know why…'

Lord, she could barely speak or walk and as Lachlan lifted her up against him she did not struggle, but placed her hands around his neck and cuddled in, comforted by the smooth feel of his skin against her cheek and the beat of his heart in her ears. Dexter followed closely behind and she smiled.

Heaven!

She was there.

Alistair Elliot arrived at Belridden with a contingent of his clan that was hardly threatening, a small band of women and some elderly people. No soldiers were in sight at all, though Lachlan said that they would be camped beyond the keep.

The woman riding beside the laird had been crying, her face blotched red and she held a handkerchief to her eyes as they came within the castle proper. Callum's mother! She could tell this was so when the boy broke free and ran towards her, towards them, his family, and was enclosed in love as the strangers dismounted and folded him into their arms.

A lost child was now found! Grace saw how Mary brought her arms about Donald in response.

'Kerr.' Elliot's voice was deep as his glance scouted across his son. 'I would thank ye for the life of my oldest son.'

'Dinna thank me. It is my wife you are obliged to.'

'She can swim?' The edge of amazement was easily heard.

'She can, and just as well that she could, aye?'

'I had nae breath, Ma. She turned me over and beat it into me.' Callum's interjection was loud.

'H-Hardly beat…' Grace began, but Lachlan stopped her with the pressure of his hand as the Chief of the Elliots bent down on his knees.

'I am indebted to you, Lady Grace, and should there be any favour that you may ask of my clan, you just need say it.'

'I d-do not think I h-have one r-right now…'

'He did not mean at this moment, Grace, but as a future insurance.'

'Of c-course.' She felt the blush of blood spill across her face.

'My wife would also like to give you something,' Alistair Kerr added as he stood again and the woman with the red eyes came forward, her fingers soft when she took Grace's hand in her own.

'This is a ring I was given as a new bride, my Lady,' she began. 'A ring of great fertility, it is said, and for me it has been so as Callum is the oldest of three other children. Wear it and you shall have as many bairns as I have and as quickly.'

Slipping it on to Grace's finger, she brought her into her arms in a hug that was all gratitude. 'Thank you for the life of my son,' she whispered, before pulling back, a new stream of tears falling.

The older woman behind suddenly began a chant in a language Grace had no notion of, the words tumbling over each other in a torrent, the tempo and volume increasing as she gathered in the emotion, and finishing with her taking soil from a bag she carried and pouring it at Grace's feet. A tiny pile of black wet earth lay against the dust of the ground before the keep, seeds mixed within it.

'The grandmother of Callum says that ye are of the soil of the Elliots. She says her hearth is your hearth and her grain is your grain. She says that the next girl child born to the Elliots clan will be called Grace and that when her grandson is the great warrior that his father is, he will protect you, too.' Lachlan translated the song easily, his voice deep across the wailing keening cry of the old woman and when it was done Grace inclined her head in thanks.

Now it was Lachlan's turn. 'Your son is a brave lad too, Alistair. It was he who jumped in to the river to save the life of one of the Kerr children and without his valour another child could have easily drowned.'

Pride swelled the chest of the Chief of the Elliots. It was a giving that was not all one-sided then, Grace thought, thus an easier gratitude to bear. The tension eased palpably and

Grace took a moment to take a proper look at Callum's mother's gift.

The silver ring was engraved with a diamond pattern and encrusted with rubies, four different stones denoting great fertility. One for each child, Grace imagined, and smiled. The sheer possibility of everything was exhilarating.

Two hours later as she retched into the bowl for the second time in as many minutes, she wondered if it was the river water that had made her so sick.

Lizzie's hand across her shoulder was comforting and she was glad that Lachlan had escorted the Elliots back to their border and would not be home until at least suppertime, for she did not wish for him to see her like this.

'When I was carrying my first bairn I was sick in the same way as you are now, my Lady.'

Grace shook her head, not wanting to acknowledge any such possibility.

He needs to love me first. He needs to tell me that he loves me, that he loves us. Not just a breeding wife after all, but a loved one.

But Lizzie was having none of it. 'If the case proves true, my Lady, give the news to no one else, no one save for your husband, for there are those here that would not take kindly to the promise of Lachlan Kerr's heir.'

'Who, Lizzie? Who w-would hurt a child?' Grace remembered back to the day Lachlan had taken her into the forest to teach her the art of self-defence. He had given her the very same warning.

'His brother.' Two words. Grace felt a shiver of fear run down the spine of her back. 'If Malcolm Kerr is still alive, he would want the Belridden lands back as his own.'

Grace's heart, already hammering fast, picked up the pace again as she remembered back to the day when the one they spoke of had lost his footing and toppled into a gully beside the river at Grantley.

'I have heard talk.' Lizzie's expression was grave. 'Your husband has heard the same talk, but to protect ye will hear none of it. If he knew that I had been giving you such information…'

'I promise I will s-say nothing.'

'And ye will be careful? For the bairn's sake as well as your own?'

A wave of nausea stopped her from answering and she felt the sweat building between her breasts and under the heavy fringe of hair at her forehead.

Lord. Her lies were closing in on her and if Malcolm Kerr was found to be alive, she knew exactly the accusations that he would level at her.

Murder and deceit. And everything would be ruined.

Lachlan rode home along the forest paths after escorting the Elliot clan off his land. He rode with Connor and Ian only, the three of them picking their way silently through the glades and always wending south-west, the sun in his face as it fell towards the Cheviots, lighting the land red.

Red.

Like Grace's hair and the colour of the rubies in the ring

that the wife of Elliot had bequeathed her. For fertility? His fingers gripped tighter on the bridle and he tried to remember if she had had her woman's bleeding here in Scotland. He did not think so. He counted back the days since arriving at Belridden, for that was when he had known her first, intimately.

A little over four weeks.

Could she have fallen with child already? The secrets between them were mounting and he could do nothing. Nothing save to try to protect her.

Chapter Twelve

Grace was restless. Lachlan still was not home and it was well past the hour of ten, darkness already fallen and the land blanketed in shadow. She had come up to his room because it was higher in the tower and, lifting the leather from the window, she looked out, searching for a light and listening for the sound of horses or shouts from the guards in the ramparts as the lost soldiers returned home.

Not that they were lost exactly, for no one seemed worried save for her. It had begun to rain heavily, slanting rain accompanied by strong breezes. Dampness permeated the castle, clinging as it was to the side of a ridge and raised up enough to feel the full brunt of the gale, wrapped in the cold mists of the Borderlands. Grace brought the blanket draped loosely across her arms to make a shawl of it over her shoulders and shivered.

'Where are you, Lachlan?' she asked of the empty shadows and wished that he would come so that she could sleep.

Just sleep?

She turned the ring on her finger and smiled.

His room was a large one, a writing desk to one side full of papers and manuscripts. Ink and quills sat at the other end, and carefully placed red wax, for his seal she supposed and looked for it, determining that it must be in one of the three drawers under the table. She wondered what else he kept in there, but did not dare to open one in case someone came. Besides, her innate sense of good etiquette would hardly allow such snooping.

Instead she pulled out his chair and sat, the comfort restful and relaxing. She imagined him here, looking at the room from this particular angle, at the wooden shelves that held his swords and the cupboard for his clothes. Standing, she walked over to open the door. A number of shirts were folded inside it, as were plaids. And there at the back lay English clothes, fine clothes of velvet and brocade. Clothes from his life before this one and from the time when he had served his king in far-off places. In Acquitaine and Brittany. In the castles that had held a child king that nobody wanted, a royal minor who had brought chaos to the land of strong and greedy men.

Scotland.

Home.

She reached out and touched the linen of his sarks and felt…reassured, though when a knock came on the door she jumped back and closed the portal of the wardrobe quickly.

'Come in.' The door opened and Lizzie stood there, her face suffused with worry.

'Please, my Lady, ye need to come now, for it is dangerous to stay up here and alone. If you came down to the Great Hall, I am sure that you would be safer. In company it will be safer.'

Seeing Lizzie's obvious fright, Grace followed the woman out, then shock hit hard as a hand snaked out to connect her full on the temple and all that she felt was a whirling blackness.

'If ye keep still, no one will hurt you, my Lady.' Lizzie's voice. Close. Blending with the pain in her head and the ache in her hands, tied to a tree in the woods, and Lachlan's mistress berating the stranger in front of them.

'Kenneth MacIndoe said he would be here,' Rebecca raged. 'He said if we brought Grace Stanton here that he would come and bring the gold.'

'Well, he cannae come as he is still in York.'

'And we cannae stay past the dawn, for if anyone should find out that we brought her…'

'Hush, niece.' Lizzie held up her hands. Niece? Her niece? Rebecca was Lizzie's niece and Kenneth MacIndoe was Malcolm Kerr's servant, the man who had seen the truth of Ginny's shame. Everything she had feared was happening.

'B-but you tried to w-warn me, Lizzie?'

The quick shake of the woman's head was baffling as was the noiselessly mouthed, 'Help!'

Help against what? Against whom? When a trail of soldiers came into the glade, Grace realised that she would never escape. Nay, she had to hold her ground and hope… Hope Lachlan would come… Hope Lizzie might help… Hope that when Kenneth MacIndoe finally saw her, he would not kill her for her lies.

The world narrowed in its options and the rain set in

hard, the blanket her maid positioned across her hair no shelter at all against the cold of autumn sleet.

'We are to bring her down to the Watchlaw Castle,' a tall, red-haired man said, 'by the way of the Tyne, for it should be swollen from the rains before nightfall and will hide any sign of our passage.'

'And Belridden? What of those who are still loyal to us at the keep?'

'The others will join us in a week and then we will take it. Did ye leave the ring, Rebecca?'

'Yes.'

Ring? Her marriage ring? Grace saw that it was no longer on her finger and worry strengthened.

'Get Kerr's wife on the horse, then.'

Two soldiers dismounted and came towards her. Loosening her ropes, they threw her up on the back of a large white steed before retying her wrists to the pommel. One of them then got up behind, his arms encircling her body roughly. She tried not to lean back, tried to keep space between them, tried to stay as still as possible as the horse moved on.

This was no moment to let her unease of riding run rampant. With Lachlan she had felt safe enough to express fear. With this man she stiffened and bit down on protest.

An owl called out in the forest, once, twice and then three times. The group stilled, tilting their heads towards the sound and pulling out swords.

Don't let it be Lachlan, Grace prayed. Please do not let it be him, for she knew he rode with two others only and this group numbered well above thirty. Even he could not win against such numbers.

There was a sound of breaking twigs and the rustle of leaves and then Dexter's face poked through the last row of small saplings, his bark of joy loud as he saw her and rushed to her side, warm, alive, the lolling red of his tongue against her shoes.

The laughter of her captors cut the tension and she was pleased when the dark-haired man who was the leader gestured for them to move on, the dog forgotten in the mêlée. With care she turned and watched him follow, her only friend amongst these strangers.

Within an hour they laboured under high cliffs of limestone and Grace knew that this was nowhere near the edge of the Kerrs' land, nowhere near the place where her husband had shepherded the Elliots from his holding. Feeling for the rosary in her pocket, she began to recite the words of salvation beneath her breath.

Lachlan held Grace's ring in his hand and swore soundly as the warmth of his skin infused into the coldness of gold. His wife had left him. When Duncan had recovered from a knock on the head, he said that Grace had gone of her own accord, walking from the keep after dark into the forest to the west, the hood of her dark blue cape pulled up. Hiding truth. Not just Grace, either, but a dozen of his men and they had carried her clothes in a heavy trunk between them.

Malcolm's supporters!

Could the mounting rumours about his brother's re-emergence be true? And if Malcolm had lived after Grantley, why had he not come back to Belridden to claim his Lairdship?

Two answers surfaced. He was ashamed at the discovery of his liaison with his brother's wife, Ruth, and the repercussions that might bring, and he had often seen his Lairdship of Belridden as a trap. But why hide and why send Kenneth MacIndoe back to the Borderlands in his stead?

Because of its connection to Grace?

Anger and hurt consumed him. What sort of a woman had he married? How could he have been so duped? A liar? A cheat?

He laid his face in his hands and breathed deeply, trying in the chaos to find a way forwards. There were many of the clan at Belridden who saw her now as a saviour, an angel, a woman who was becoming more and more like one of their own, and when he had left he was certain that Grace had been happy, the Elliots' praise in front of everyone all that she had striven for since being here.

Damn.

Nothing made sense, but there was no sign of a struggle, no reason to believe she had not gone by choice. One of her shifts lay in a ball against the end board of their bed, dropped in the hurry of exit, he determined, as he picked it up. Delicate and lacy, it smelled of Grace. Flowers and the essence of woman. Swallowing hard, he dropped the thing in the fire where it went up in a welt of flame and smoke.

Ephemeral and transient! The whole impermanence of his life suddenly overcame him; never a place or a home or a person that was truly his. Never trust or honesty or faith.

Like these flames, burning bright and then gone, only smoke and soot left. Another thought made him stiffen. She had taken the dog, too, for it no longer hung in the room or about the Great Hall, its golden eyes watching his wife's every move.

He wished that there could have been a battle tomorrow, a skirmish where he could just leave his sword at his side and ride into oblivion.

But there would not be.

Nay, tomorrow he would have to face his people and tell them in the best way that he could why his wife of a month had packed up her things and left him. He did not even want to think about another of Malcolm's betrayals.

Grace shivered as she gathered up her hair with her one free hand, the dank wetness of it away from her neck making her realise just how cold she had become. Everything was wet. Her body, her feet, the blanket she had around her and the muddy ground beneath her. But at least there had been no sign of Kenneth MacIndoe and for that she was glad. Dexter hung in the shadows of the trees and away from the light. She heard him growl sometimes, a dark shape at the edge of the clearing and, although pieces of meat had been flung to him, he ignored them, his eyes glued on Grace. She did not know whether she wanted him to stay or go, because surely it would soon be obvious to those who held her that this was her dog, and then they might hurt him.

Others had joined the party two nights ago, Englishmen,

and the one who was their leader seemed increasingly interested in her person. 'Lord Thomas' was his name and she
had seen him looking at her all throughout this day, the
gleam in his eyes dangerous and undecipherable.

Everything of value had been stripped from her, save her
rosary and the stone deep in the pocket of her gown. Even
her shoes had been replaced by rough leather brogans that
were at least a size too big. Another woman now wore her
shoes, though she had noticed the way the girl had hobbled
before bedding down tonight, the sturdier leather obviously
blistering her heels.

A small revenge.

The thought made her smile.

'Ye seem happy, my Lady.' The man they named Paul
the Black sidled up next to her, placing his hand lewdly
across the top of her thigh. This caused Lord Thomas to
stand and join them.

'She isn't to be handled by the likes of you,' he said, his
hand on the hilt of the sword in his belt, and the growling
at the edge of the clearing became louder.

Others about him stood, a circle of bristling men. She was
the only one who could not rise.

'I've seen the way ye look at her, Thomas, the way ye
notice the curves of her.' Simon pulled out his own
sword, waving it in the face of the other. 'And if ye can't
control the itch you are beset with, then perhaps I can
scratch it for you.'

A torrent of Gaelic made some men laugh, and made the
faces of others darken. Not an easy alliance then, Grace

surmised, for what greed brought together it could also rip asunder.

Without notice another man moved up behind her, blade out across the line of her throat. For a moment she thought that he might have actually cut deep, but then after a few seconds she realised that she still breathed.

'Come closer and I will kill her,' he shouted, pulling up her hair and snipping the length of it before holding it up. Like a trophy or a prize! 'If ye let her womanhood seduce ye, the battle that is ahead for all of us will be lost. This is about the fight for land that is rightfully ours, you understand. Bickering amongst ourselves will bring our cause no further than the useless spilling of blood.'

The shape of black leapt, followed by a quick flash of white teeth and a howl of rage from the man who held her, his blade now turned to Dexter, slashing into the space between them as Grace fell, her head whipped against the trunk of a tree and stars forming. Others joined to quell the dog, longer swords prodding at his hindquarters.

Grace could not stop any of it. Her world turned in dizziness, the sounds fainter now as she tried to breathe, tried to help him, her dog who fought them all without a thought for his own safety. The rope bit into her wrists as she kicked out and her trophy of curls scattered in the mud where her attacker had dropped them.

Tears of relief and fright blinded her as Dexter broke free and disappeared into the forest in that particular lolling gait he had. Not too hurt, then? She put up her one free hand and felt the short nothingness of hair plastered to her scalp.

Uglier still, though the faces of those men who watched her suggested the opposite.

Lizzie stood watching through the gloom and Grace looked away. If only Dexter could find his way home, then Lachlan would come. To save her.

Lachlan cursed as he learned of the number of men massing on the border of his land. Englishmen and Scotsmen, though he had heard no whisper that his brother was amongst them. Was Grace there, too, or had she gone south to Grantley to meet Malcolm? It was all a puzzle; if, indeed, his brother was alive, he could not just walk back into Belridden and expect to rule it. Some here would support him, but there were three times as many who would not and there was no way he could claim Grace in marriage. Unless Lachlan was dead!

I love you.

Grace had said it to him whilst she slept once and he had held her until the morning light came, just them and a feeling unlike any other he had ever felt.

She could not have lied. She could not have feigned that sleepily whispered promise.

Two days since she had gone and he missed her more with every passing minute.

Please God let her be safe. Let her live. Let Malcolm be kind to her if it was to him she had run. All he wanted was to see her again, to look into her eyes and know that she had chosen the path she had taken willingly, because what if…?

What if she had been taken against her will? The bruises on her arm and legs were still not healed from the rescue at the river and when she was scared she stuttered more. Stuttered so much that some might lose patience? He made himself stop, swallowing back fear and panic. Nay, Duncan had seen her leave, walking from Belridden of her own accord and in the company of those who had remained loyal to his brother. She had left her ring and taken her clothes, and the notes in the jewelled box suggested she had loved Malcolm with a passion. It was that simple and to believe anything else was foolish.

Lachlan readied his keep for war and sent riders to Edinburgh and David by way of Liddesdale and Kelso. And when that was done, he called his retainers together in the Great Hall, waiting for the noise of those before him to settle until he began to speak.

'This castle has been divided by the wants of greedy men.' There was silence. 'Scotland has been divided by the wants of greedy men. Almost forty years ago forty Scottish nobles affixed their seals to a declaration promising freedom. Freedom against the lordship of the English. Do we have it now? Do we have it today here at Belridden where the echoes of the Bruce's legacy still linger?' He waited and tried to catch the eyes of those who would support Malcolm. 'The English have amassed their own force on the border near Whitelee and they want to take the Borderlands into English ownership. Balliol's supporters, the disinherited ones.' His hand fell upon his sword, calling to arms those whose allegiances hung in a different camp from his own. There was silence. 'I can tell you right here and now that unless we fight, Scotland will never be free. Unless we know that here in our hearts, in our hearths, in the land beneath our feet and our ancestors' feet that it is an independent and strong Scotland that we seek, we shall never truly be Scots.' He waited as the words distilled, a touch in the air of something he could only guess to be akin to kingship, of leading men where you may will them, and of seeing in the choices a right and proper path. 'Are ye with me?' He raised his sword high above his head, liking how the light from the arched windows fell upon steel, the shadow of war drawn upon the floor of his keep in a powerful image. Aye, he was enough of a diplomat to believe in the significance of turning the tide and enough of a soldier to treat the sentiment with caution. There was never certainty when one tried to bend the will of many and he waited.

Simon McLeod was the first to challenge him. 'Your brother ruled the keep for years. You have barely been here. If he is alive, perhaps his claim to the land is the rightful one.'

'My brother ruled as a man who wanted the clans around us vanquished.'

'Replaced with those who fought with Balliol more like,' another shouted. Connor. Lachlan dipped his head in thanks.

'If those who lost land under Bruce were to reclaim their lands, the English would have an easy route into Scotland. It would not just be the disinherited that we had as neighbours. It would be those from further south, those with the support of Edward the Third of England and with the strength of his army.'

'And what of Stewart and Douglas? What of the strength of their armies if we throw our lot in with David's court?'

'They have interests only in the north and the west. Their power should not worry us here.'

'I vote that we draw a line,' Ian yelled across the conversation of those deciding just where their allegiances lay. 'I vote that those with Lachlan stay on this side and those against cross over.'

Lachlan nodded; taking his sword, he fashioned a mark, past the feet of the last retainer in the empty space at the end of the Hall. And deliberately stepped back across it.

No one moved, swords in their scabbards and hands by their sides.

'Verra well, then.' His voice was softer now, filled with an emotion that was foreign to him.

Home. Here. After all these years of wandering. 'We will leave Belridden in the morning and make for England.'

'*Belleden*,' one voice cried, the battle call of the Kerrs resounding about the keep in the answer of all those present. A commotion outside caught their attention; when the doors to the hall opened, the Elliot soldiers filed in one by one and bereft of weaponry.

'We are here to help you retrieve your wife,' Alistair Elliot said finally when the procession had at last come to a halt. 'A priest from Annan came to our lands yesterday and told us of her capture.'

'Capture?' Lachlan's answer was weary and cold, a tight shot of suspicion edged in anger.

'He saw her, the Lady Grace, ye understand, with her

hands tied and her face marked in a camp to the south, and if he had not come down with the sickness he would be here telling you the same thing.'

'Grace has been hurt?' Lachlan's bellow rattled the cups stacked on a table behind him. 'Someone has hurt her?'

The constriction that tightened his throat threatened to choke him. She had not gone willingly to the camp of his enemies? The pain of relief drew down upon him, scratching at the greasier surface of betrayal.

'The priest tells me that your wife is alive, Laird Kerr. He tried to persuade them to let her go under the banner of Christian charity, but they would have none of it.'

A vision of Grace injured swam into the red boiling wrath of his vengeance. She hated horses and was always cold, and without medicine the chafing of her skin would be much worsened. The rain outside slanted in from the north, a freezing icy blast that had taken hold of the Borderlands for almost three days now and it would be all of two more until he could reach her.

An inconceivable impotence had him frozen to the spot, the beat of his heart pounding in his ears and ire making it hard to say anything.

Grace. Hurt. Scared. Shocked.

With care he raised his sword from its sheath and held it upwards. An answer to a prayer! The final absolution!

'To England,' he roared, all the hate and enmity in the words provoking a great shout as clans who had despised each other changed before his very eyes.

Because of Grace and her goodness.

The hilt of his sword was held so hard that his fingers began to shake as he calculated in the numbers that surrounded him, at least a chance to bring her back.

Chapter Thirteen

His brother was nowhere amongst the party. Lachlan could see that as soon as the line rode forwards, see it in the standards of the banners and the colours on the painted shields.

More than two hundred men were behind the leading group of ten, and less than a hundred and fifty retainers grouped on his own side. Con, Ian, Marcus, Kenneth, Duncan. Alistair. Good men. His men. King David's supporters for whom the Berwick Treaty had delivered only an empty promise of peace. Elliot's words mirrored his own.

'It seems someone has mustered English help and plenty of it. Half as many again as ours if I were to take a guess at the numbers.'

'We have an advantage, coming from the higher ground,' Lachlan returned and liked the way the Laird of the Elliot clan laughed.

'Aye, that we have.'

He turned then to raise his arm, and steadily the lines moved forwards, shields at the ready and swords honed sharp. Then they gave the horses their heads and raced into battle.

* * *

A knife sliced away the binding of ropes at her hands and Grace was aroused from her dozing.

'Lizzie?'

'Hurry or they will be back, my Lady.'

Lack of blood in her fingers had made them fat and numb and she shook them out and winced as pain replaced dullness. A soldier lay opposite, a streak of blood trailing its way through the darkness of his hair.

'Is he d-dead?'

'I dinna think so, but I cannae be sure, mind, for I hit him hard. What I do know is that when he awakens he will shout out warning.'

'You would s-save me over th-them?'

'I came only to help you and this is the first chance that I have had to do so. Now come, we must be away before they know us gone.'

The trail they took ran into the woods behind them and then doubled up around the hill to a clearing. Thick bush lay to one side and to the other…the field of war, uneven battle lines drawn in the green and the true sharp aim of swords bright in the thin sun.

Lachlan was there. Right there, his life as tied to deceit as her own. With a growing panic she gestured Lizzie to halt.

'No. I cannot go on. Not yet.'

'But we cannae stop either, my Lady,' she returned, 'for we need to get as far away as we can, otherwise everything I have pretended will be in vain.'

'But if my husband is hurt…'

'Then we will all be dead,' the small woman said and grabbed at her arm.

But Grace would not be budged. 'Please, Lizzie, just give me a moment.' She thought she might be sick, a wave of biliousness making her sweat, and she reached a shaking hand to her forehead. 'I have to stop for a moment.'

Watch and listen and know.

Her glance again went towards the grouped opponents, the ring of swords and the shriek of horses, Lachlan's red-and-green blazon fluttered above mayhem and bedlam and anarchy. Still aloft. She searched for his brother's matching standard, but could not find it. Perhaps Malcolm Kerr had not come at all. Perhaps the rumours were only that. Perhaps her husband might win on that field of carnage even with such numbers stacked against him.

'Please, please let that be.' Her fingers passed across the face of the burnished Argus moth in amber and also the solid beads of her rosary. Pagan gods and Catholic incantations. She left no part of it to chance as she invoked her needed help from a divergent source of deities.

For a while he held out against the flash of steel and dagger, the charge of his horse and the retreat of those about him. Aye, for a while she saw what made him the King's champion knight, the only one who refused to partake in the tournaments and was not challenged for it. For a while the bodies about the destrier of the man riding behind the shield of red and green grew and grew. Unmoving. Ominous. But he could not fight them all, wave upon wave, and his voice was audible from where she stood.

'Pog mo thon, a mhic an diabhoil!'

From the reaction of those around him, Grace supposed this to be a serious Gaelic curse, for if anything the fighting intensified, as the ears of those he fought interpreted the slur in a way that she could not.

Hope dashed as his standard fell, down through the cantons and pales and saltires of all colours, down through the mêlée of horses' hooves, to the ground, mace and hammer and falchion prodding at his mail and armour, stopping only as the strapped wrapper of his coif ripped from the polished helm and dark black hair was strewn on to rolling green.

A great cheer went up, echoing through the ranks of his opponents and Grace ran, shaking off Lizzie's arm, ran through the grass and across the field to the place he had fallen, the shape of others only peripheral, flail and mace as nothing to stop her reaching the one man whom she sought.

Lachlan.

He struggled with breath and the blood from beneath his aventail dripped on to the skirt of her cape. Bending, she rolled him over to one side where perhaps he could take the air that he needed.

Panic settled full when he did not and she shook him until he coughed, spittle and blood, thick, formed across his face.

'Take her.' A voice from behind, the cadence of it familiar. Malcolm Kerr. There was a whirring slap of leather and her hands were tied, the wooden pommel of a falchion catching her unawares and then all she knew was the rust-sharp taste of blood.

* * *

'She has woken.'

Grace heard the words through a haze of white. Opening her eyes, she saw she was in a well-appointed room, pictures of angels above her. Angels. Was she dead? When the pain struck her arm, she knew that she wasn't and caught her breath. Two women beside her looked worried. They wore nuns' habits, each with a gold cross dangling from their necks.

'Keep still. I am bleeding you.'

She did as she was told, trying to speak, trying to ask, trying to form a name in her mind, but she could not.

Lachlan?

She wondered why she could not, and with her tongue, explored the outside of her lip on the left side. It was swollen sore.

'I have stitched your arm where the blade hit it. There will be a mark there.'

'Laird Lachlan Kerr? Is he safe?'

Silence. Grace knew the moment that nobody spoke that he was lost. She turned from them, from the eyes that could measure her grief. Her husband dead. The only man she would ever love. Nothing left of any of it.

When she woke again it was night. A single candle burnt beside the bed, shadow pushed away.

'Gracie?'

Judith sat beside her, her smile and voice soft, and a look in her face that hardly knew how to say what she thought.

I am so very sorry.

For the first time in this room of angels Grace felt tears coursing down her cheeks, wetting the sheets and the bandage, her body shrunk into regret, hope flown like the cherubs hovering above her, wings lifting them up, into another place, a softer place. The place that Lachlan had gone to? The very best of the King's knights surely should have a rest in Heaven that was finally easy?

'You have been here for almost six days.'

'Here?'

'A nunnery just outside Eddington. Malcolm Kerr held a meeting with Stephen and Father yesterday.'

Lord, so he was alive. She had not imagined his voice.

'Why?'

Her cousin tucked her hand in her lap. 'You need to get well first, Grace. You need to eat again for you are so thin…'

'Why?' She repeated the question again, waiting for the right answer.

'He said that he would still consider you as a bride.'

Horror spiralled, choking her with the dreadful certainty of the man's cleverness.

He wanted her money and he would get it because Stephen and her uncle would have no way to counteract his plans without ruining them all.

'I c-cannot…'

'I know, but until we can think of a way to get you out of here we need him to believe that you will. He is a powerful force, with friends in high places and the ear of Edward. His mission north has been hailed as a triumph.'

'His standard was not th-there, he c-came only at the e-end…'

'Go to sleep. I'll stay beside you, I promise.'

'And U-Uncle…?'

'Is speaking with the King to ask if you could stay here at the nunnery.'

'For ever and ever.' Grace could not even contemplate the very length of it as she closed her eyes and dreamed.

They were in the cave, a shadow cave. Neither Belridden. Nor Grantley. Not the soft mist of the north nor the damp of this lower lying city. Lighter. Warmer.

'Je t'aime toujours.'

French. I will love you, always. French as fluent as one raised there, his hand across hers…

No, that was not right. Nothing left. A moth in amber in her fingers laughing, an argus moth and double banded.

For luck, Donald had said. Just for luck.

Good? Bad? She had not asked.

'Grace. Grace.' Her uncle's voice. The heaviness of her eyelids and then his face over her and worried.

'We are here with you. There was a battle and you were hurt…'

Killed. Dead. Lachlan's face turned away with the spittle of blood. In that one horrible second everything that had happened came back. She could not catch breath with the grief of it.

'I have spoken with Edward of England. He wants to meet you and find out what your wishes are.'

'My w-wishes?'

'For your future.'

A future. Grace could barely think about getting through the next hour, let alone a whole future. She shook her head and resolution firmed.

'I wish to st-stay at G-Grantley. If it is marriage to M-Malcolm Kerr he is thinking of…'

The guilt that covered her uncle's cheeks was telling. 'If there is any way Ginny could be spared…'

Grace held her hand up and he stopped.

Her life was ruined already and Ginny's was just beginning. But to marry Malcolm Kerr… No, she could not do it. Would not do it. Even for Ginny.

'I can p-pay Kerr off. The dowry is all he wanted in the f-first place and if it is offered free of any conditions…'

Her uncle nodded. 'We can try.'

The headache that had been threatening throbbed now. Lachlan's face smeared in blood and stains from the field on to which he had fallen. Where was his body now?

'Were p-prisoners held as ransom?'

'Yes, by the English. They are at Watchlaw Castle, awaiting repayments from their vassals.'

For the first time a quiver of something akin to hope surged in Grace's breast. Watchlaw. A castle not far from Eddington.

'Could you arrange f-for me to see them? I need to f-find out what happened—' She stopped.

'I could try, though I have seen the list and Lachlan Kerr is not numbered amongst them.' Grace squeezed her uncle's hand when he held it out and prayed to God for a miracle.

* * *

Lachlan pulled at the ropes on his leg and cursed the English bastards who had sent him here.

Connor's condition had worsened, and one of the Elliot soldiers brought in with their group had a gaping wound on his thigh that was untended and weeping.

Lachlan shouted out for the hundredth time that day, 'Bring medicine, you English dogs, for there are those here who are ill.'

His own shoulder ached. He had tried to look at it, but had given up, the effort required not worth the pain, and brackish water all that was left to tend it. Looking across at Ian, he saw the same anger in his eyes that he was certain must be in his own.

'It seems as if we have been forgotten. Perhaps your brother has counselled the English so. Or your wife?'

He had heard Grace had been seen in Malcolm's arms after the battle, entwined in each other like the lovers she had purported them not to be, and the pure rage that consumed Lachlan still lingered.

Betrayed when he had thought her to be so true? What constancy lay in any of it? Another feckless wife! He tried not to care, for there were other matters more pressing. They had not seen Duncan or Alistair Elliot since yesterday afternoon and Lachlan wondered where the hell it was they had gone. The first sacrifices? He kept his fears to himself. 'David will no doubt send missives negotiating our return.'

'Aye, but will they come in time?' Ian looked pointedly down at the gaping hole on the Elliot soldier's thigh and

Lachlan shook away worry. They had been here by his reckoning for nigh on ten days and every single piece of clothing worth something had been taken from them. Sitting barefoot in thin sarks on a cold stone floor, he was blindingly aware of the losses they had suffered.

Lord, they would die here in the hands of the English behind bars in the gloom and be buried…where? He was just about to shout again when keys rattled from further out.

Bates, the jailer, stepped through, a mace in hand, the wicked steel on its spikes showing hair and skin where some unlucky recipient had strayed too close.

'You've a visitor. Make sharp.'

Considering their ankles were bound to the wall and their hands tied, Lachlan did his best not to smile. He had done so yesterday at some other order that the man had given and felt the damage on his neck. Better to shut up and wait for a chance. Was this it? He unfolded his body and leaned back against the stone, a light-headed dizziness overtaking all other intent. God, when had they last been fed? The day before yesterday or the day before that again?

Grace stepped into the dim like a princess, her hair covered with a burgundy scarf and the russet cape she wore swirling with fine fur, and if her face was pale it now paled further, ashen pallid. Her eyes were huge pools of darkness against a chalky countenance as she saw him, just a spark of question and then rolling back in her head, the small cry of his name barely audible as she simply crumpled, down, down to a floor filthy with rushes and dust and silence.

Lach pulled with all his might against the rope, against the futility of capture and hurt and bondage as his wife lay like a doll ten yards from him, her body strangely thinner. What the hell had just happened? He shouted her name loud, until the mace came down, shoving good sense across bad, the sound of his breath ragged and frenzied, the tang of fear choking panic.

And then she was gone, lifted by the jailer, carelessly, he thought.

And gone.

The clang of the door, the fading of light and then darkness.

'Gun toireach an diabhul fhein leis anns a bhas sibh, direach di Ifrinn!' His curse followed them into the silence, echoing around stone—*'Ifrinn, Ifrinn, Ifrinn'*—back and back to him as if some unholy ghost played games with his dread. Then quiet, his breath the only noise in the gloom.

'What's ye wife…doing here?' Con's voice was weakened from his malady.

'More to the point, will she be back?' he answered and hoped like hell that Bates was not hurting her. Why had she come alone and at darkness and where was Malcolm?

Alive. Lachlan was alive. Alive, not under his name but that of Angus MacIndoe. She checked the list of the Scottish prisoners as she recovered in the room Bates held as his own, a drink of mead in her hand and a smile that confused him.

Lord. When had she become so good at deceit? The faint. The blade. The smile. The added use of her stutter to make the man opposite give her a look that was almost…fatherly.

'I c-c-cannot understand wh-wh-what came o-over me.'

'The dungeons do that to anyone and your uncle should be hanged for letting you come down here alone.'

She slipped him another coin from her purse to keep him talking.

'Usually the knights from battle would be ransomed, but these ones are to hang the day after tomorrow.'

Grace felt her throat constrict with fear. 'C-Could they b-be released if e-enough m-money was p-paid?'

The man stood still. Calculating, Grace reasoned. Calculating his risk and her ability to pay. Finally he shook his head.

'Three prisoners could not just disappear…'

When he stopped, she saw the glint of something that she knew could be dangerous. With a smile she placed her cup on the table and stood. Push him too far and he would talk to those she did not want him to.

'Th-thank y-you. I shall f-find my uncle and l-leave.'

'And if anyone asks after you, what exactly should I say?'

Grace pushed more coinage across the table.

'Say n-nothing.'

Time stretched out, one hour and then two, the snores of the others telling Lach that they were asleep. He moved carefully and stood so as not to make a noise and alert Con or Ian to anything of difference, and with his foot reached out and out towards the blade his wife had dropped unseen as she fell, the small silver of it just visible under a pile of rushes.

He could not have planned it better himself, the crumpled

faint and the careful letting go of what was in her hand. None had seen but him. Finally he had a foothold, an edge of the dagger, its hilt turning so that he could catch it with his toe, the lack of brogans an unexpected benefit. Stooping, he picked it up, the sharp edge of steel against rope, then freedom. No restraints. He rubbed at the tight prickling numbness at his wrists, thinking.

By the morning light Lachlan had formed a plan. He would take Bates when he came with the water at midday. A corpse could hardly stay inside a cell—the fetid smell of the decaying flesh of the Elliot soldier was all-encompassing—the groans that had punctuated the night had stopped. Bates would have to come in and this knife gave him an edge of surprise. If they did not take this chance, there would never be another one. He was sure of it. Eleven days and no visitors save for his wife, and Duncan and Alistair and the others lost to them.

Ian had seen the blade when he woke and his eyebrows had risen and fallen again with Lachlan's gesture of silence. Too far to reach across and cut his bonds with these fetters around his ankles, fetters he did not dare to slice in case Bates saw such freedom before turning the key. The moments stretched into mid-morning, relentlessly slow.

Grace came as he was snoozing, catching up from the lost sleep from the night before. He opened his eyes and she was there, watching him, her cape this morning of white velvet and again she wore a scarf.

'I'm not certain that this is a good idea, my Lady.' Bates's voice.

'It is only a cr-cross of g-gold and I should just like to place one each around their necks b-before…' She stopped and wiped her eyes with a dainty kerchief. Lachlan could see no sign at all of tears.

'Then in and out in a second. Do not tarry.'

She stepped through the door and started towards Lachlan, a look in her eyes he had never seen there before. Commanding. Forceful. Trying to communicate with her eyes what she wanted him to do.

She passed the slingshot to him under the cover of the cape and he took it, notching the stone even before she had stepped away. It flew through the bars and between the eyes of Bates, who did not see it coming.

'The keys.'

She ran to get them, placing them in his fingers with surprisingly steady hands before leaving the cell to pick up a bag. Monks' robes and sandals, fine leather and warm wool spilled out on to the filthy stone floor.

'W-We have about f-four more minutes before another guard comes. I counted the w-watches yesterday.'

She watched as he dressed Con. 'C-Can he walk?'

'Yes.' He gave her the answer that he wanted rather than the truth, but he could not leave Connor here to the mercy of the English. Donald would be waiting for him, and Mary with the new bairn who had not seen even one full year.

Slinging his friend across his shoulder, he followed Grace out, dagger in hand. Ian brought up the rear with the slingshot and a pocketful of stones. These would have to be enough as they walked, his wife taking this corner and that passage and all about them the living and breathing wetness of stone.

It could not be long until they were stopped, for in the distance he could make out voices. Grace seemed to hear none of it, intent on gaining the outside. For the first time he had followed her he did not notice a limp.

'H-Here. It is h-here.'

They slipped into a small room, a jug of mead on the table. Waiting, she gestured quiet and the hammer of feet passed by them after a moment.

'N-Now we must just run.'

There was no finesse as they careened down the corridors and into a larger yard to the shouts of soldiers and the first real opposition. Sitting Con down against a wall and gesturing his wife to stay with him, Lachlan took the knife in hand. He made short work of the first two and Ian finished off the last one.

Grabbing Con again, they negotiated a room full of laundry and then another room largely empty. Two more moments and they were through an unprotected gate and outside, four horses waiting tethered to a rail, an urchin looking up in relief.

'Thought you were not comin'.' He held out his hand to receive a coin and scampered off. Lachlan passed the inert form of Con up to Ian before turning back to Grace.

'Your turn.'

She shook her head. 'I was n-never coming. It would be far more dangerous to t-take me and my family is here...'

He pulled her to him, anger giving the movement more than an edge of roughness. 'Think again, my lady wife, for I was never going to leave you.'

Chapter Fourteen

Up on the horse the same old panic claimed her, but this time Lachlan seemed to be prepared, his arms hiking her full up against his body and leaving hardly a space between them.

'I h-have organised more horses to be w-w-waiting in Murton.'

He ignored her completely, tying off the bridle of the spare mount and proceeding in exactly the opposite direction that she had indicated.

'It is not this way…'

'Forgive me if I do not follow your pathway, but I feel it wiser to lay out my own escape route.'

'I d-don't understand.'

'It is said that you left the battlefield in the arms of my brother.'

Suddenly she saw it all. The anger and the suspicion. Did he think this had been her doing? If she had been less afraid of being on a horse she might have hit him, but her hands were too busy with the action of just clinging on.

'Y-You would th-think th-that of me?'

'Enough, Grace. If the minions of Edward catch us up, you can explain that you tried to send me in their direction and I shall not correct you. That I will do for the blade and these steeds. But for now stay quiet, aye.'

She felt his thighs tighten around her own in a silent warning and with the wind in her face and the bruises and dried blood caking his arm and hands she felt it prudent to obey.

He thought she had betrayed him, thought that she had run to Malcolm and the English. Well, she would not tell him the true way of it, would not say. Not here. Not now. Not with the law at their heels and the tone in his words distant and removed.

'He's out, Lach.' Ian's shout, as Connor's head lolled to one side.

Lachlan slowed the pace. 'Are ye able to hold him?'

'For now.'

'Ravenwood is within easy distance of here. If we can get him there in time, Justin will help us.'

His voice was low and Grace saw that he unstrapped the monk's belt he wore at his waist. 'Take this and tie his hand to yours. At least that way if he falls you'll have some measure of control and if he goes over…'

'He will nae.'

'Good.'

They did not speak again, the quick glances between the two men becoming more and more numerous as the hour went on.

Finally, a house came into sight. She took in breath at the sheer and utter wealth of the lines of stone, and the dozens of servants fanning out from an enormous frontage. To greet them? Almost as if they had been expected?

'Who l-lives here?'

'Justin, the Duke of Ravenwood, and his wife, Celeste.' The tone of his voice told her a lot more than the words. These people were important to him.

Surreptitiously, Grace tried to straighten her headrail and smooth out the wilted folds of her skirt.

He was blind! The Duke of Ravenwood was blind. She could see it as his hand slid across Lachlan Kerr's shoulder, searching, outlining skin and bone, the long stroke of his fingers forming a picture and moving upwards along the planes of his face.

'You have been hurt.'

Lachlan stepped back and tipped his head to the woman standing beside the Duke. 'Celeste. It has been a long time.'

'Too long.' She enfolded him to her, like a mother might, or a lover. There were undertones that Grace could not understand. Finally they parted, tears evident on the sooty lashes of the Duke's wife.

'We had heard that you were dead.' Her French accent was strong. 'John Murray was here two days ago on his way to London and David is furious.'

'Malcolm is alive, Lach.' Justin Ravenwood's eyes, scarred in whiteness, looked straight at Grace. He knew who she was without any introduction and without being able to see her? She frowned. His wife would have given him her description and it could hardly be flattering.

Suddenly everything seemed dangerous. These people, Lachlan's anger, and murky politics that held resurgents accountable for everything.

Judith and her uncle must be worried sick at her being gone, for she had not let them know where she was. Home. Family. Things she knew and trusted. So unlike here. She would send a missive to them from Ravenwood for she still had coinage in her pocket.

Everything was difficult and she longed to simply step over and take her husband's hand in her own, in the hope that he might take it back, blending the grief of loss and hurt into care. But he was distracted by Con's sickness and Ian's worry and the mention of his brother. He crossed the room away from her to take the weight of Connor on to his own shoulders.

'Do you have a physician on hand, Justin?'

'We do, though you will need to bring him through. My wife tells me you wear the robe of a monk, so perhaps if the mantle of religion has come upon you now would be a good time to pray.'

'My father cured me of that, and you of all people should ken it so.'

Their voices faded and Grace was left with Celeste, myriad servants staring at her from their places around the well-appointed salon.

'I presume without the benefit of introduction you are Lady Grace Stanton, Lachlan's new wife?'

Grace nodded. 'By the o-order of two k-kings.'

'A less than salubrious start then. No wonder Lach looks on you as the enemy.'

Shock resonated through Grace. Was his hatred of her so very easy to fathom, so transparent that this woman could see it in the few moments that her guest had been here? Not knowing how to answer, she kept quiet.

'I was Lachlan's lover at the Chateau-Gaillard in France.'

'And th-then Justin's?' Two could play at this game and Grace had suddenly had enough.

Unexpectedly the other woman laughed. 'I was begin-ning to think that you were as the court has said it, and I am glad to see that that is not the case.'

'Timid?'

'No, proper! A woman of conventional manners and refined sedateness. So sedate, in fact, that one could throw any insult and be merely smiled at.'

'I used to be like th-that until…'

'Until?'

'Until I m-married Lachlan Kerr.'

'He is a good lover, no?'

The blush seemed to start at her feet and rise upwards and she furtively cast a glance at the servants who were within easy hearing distance.

'How old are you, Grace?'

'Twenty-six.' A shameful age to admit she still blushed, but there it was. She wished she dared ask the same question of the woman opposite, but if she were younger than she was, everything would again be so much worse.

'I am thirty-three.'

Grace nodded, her head spinning with the vague and uneasy notion that this woman was a mind-reader.

'My husband was one of Edward's most trusted advisers.'

'W-Was?'

'Politics took more from Justin than he wanted to give, so he left it in the hands of those who were brutal enough to stand it and retired to the country.'

'But us c-coming here will involve you…'

'Oh, that is completely different. We have always been involved in Lach's life.'

With a single click of her fingers Celeste dismissed the servants and waited until the room was cleared.

'Might I give you a warning, Grace? Your husband has been chased by all of the most beautiful women in Europe and he has not needed to work for any of it. Make him pursue you. Make him wonder. Make him understand that without you his life would be as nothing.'

Grace's heart began to thump. Was this woman mad? Cornflower-blue eyes keenly watched her.

'Lachlan has been as the seed of a dandelion all of his life. Blown this way and that way by politics and by war. Scotland. England. France. All have been his place of rest, but never a home. My advice to you would be to make him that, Grace, a home.'

'You would help me? Why?'

'Because you are a good woman and you are strong. You will need to be strong.'

She could say no more as the men reappeared, the servants behind carrying hot water and bathing sheets.

'We have placed you in the rooms at the top of the stairs.' There was a trace of something in the Duchess of Ravenwood's tone that was unusual and Grace wished she were away from these people and their words with hidden meanings. She also wondered why her husband had not so much as glanced at her ever since arriving at the Ravenwood mansion.

'I will stay with Connor for a while, Celeste, but I am certain that my wife would appreciate a bath.'

'If you would like to follow me then, Lady Kerr, I will show you to your room.'

The moon lay low on the horizon as Grace watched it much later. She had bathed and eaten and still Lachlan had not returned. She was just wondering whether or not she should get into bed and sleep when she heard sounds of movement from the room next to hers. Holding her breath, she laid her ear against the wall, trying better to decipher the sounds. Could this be where Lachlan slept? Were these adjoining chambers? She remembered Celeste's humour when she had told him of the sleeping arrangements. Perhaps because this way he would have a choice of lying with her...or not.

When a door at the far end of the room opened to admit him, she was surprised. And surprised again when she saw what it was he wore. No longer the Highland sark and plaid, but shirt and hose and an embroidered cotehardie with wide sleeves.

'It was a choice between Justin's English clothes or the monk's habit.' The tone told her that neither would have been his first option, though she had little time to think on this as he strode forwards and took one of her thin arms in his hand.

'God, have ye nae been fed since last I saw you?' The

contact was not sensual or carnal, but merely the touch of one who would know the way of things.

'Not much, my Lord.' The sound of her voice was husky and his eyes flicked to her head.

'And have you taken to wearing headgear to bed?'

Her hands went uncertainly to the fabric covering what little was left of her hair and he cursed again as her chin tipped up to the light. 'Who did this?'

The wound of the knife had never properly healed and Grace knew it to be a red welt across the paleness of her throat.

'The s-same man w-who d-did this,' she returned and undid the veil, the shortness of her hair reflected in the frown on her husband's face. 'Though it was a s-service he did me, in truth, f-for I was about to be raped by another.' She saw that he balled his hands into fists.

'Malcolm did not protect you then?''

'Your brother.' Real puzzlement showed. 'Why sh-should he do that?'

'You left the battlefield with him.'

'No. I w-was taken against my will and I did not see him in the countryside. It was only after the battle that I heard his voice before someone hit me.'

'Lord, so the words that Elliot said were true.' He stepped back, pale eyes ice cold as he ran a hand through his hair. 'It was said that you walked from Belridden in your dark blue cape and by your own accord?'

'I was b-bound and b-bundled into a trunk before being carried out by those loyal to your b-brother. Your mistress pretended to be me.'

'Rebecca?

'She wore my c-cape and the hood was up.'

The truth of it all was starting to show in his eyes.

'I t-tried to help you b-breathe when you f-f-fell but someone t-took me before I could know that you l-lived.'

'And after the battle?'

'I awoke in a c-convent a few d-days later in the attendance of my cousins and my uncle. I d-do not know wh-what happened t-t-to your brother. I understood y-you were dead when y-you did not come.'

He ignored her words as his finger touched the trail of the mark on her throat, a careful anger inherent in the action. 'You understood nothing.' The words were bleak, and she fathomed none of it, something glowing in his eyes that she could not interpret. Not fury. Nor pity. Something new. She shut her eyes against what she thought she saw. She had not felt comfort for so long that the pain of loss consumed her. Different. Everything was different now. The reddened skin on her cheeks hurt as she opened her eyes and tried to smile. Through it. Through what she knew he would now say.

'You are beautiful, Grace.'

Not that. She had not thought that. The beat of her heart squeezed in hurt and joy, mixed strangely.

'You wear the scarf because you don't think so? You think that I would care? You think that the loss of your hair should make you less to me somehow?'

One single tear fell down the length of her cheek, tracing coldness before it fell on her hand. *Make him pursue you.*

Make him wonder. Celeste's words! But how was she to do that with her ragged hair and her reddened face and a stutter that had worsened ever since arriving at Ravenwood.

Her chin wobbled and the aching sorrow at the back of her throat repressed words, though she could sense his breath on her cheeks, close. He had not moved away, then—out of sorrow or in compassion, she knew not which, but he had not moved away.

'Did you ever love my brother?'

A different question. In the baldness of what he had just told her she could no longer lie.

'No. I never l-loved him. I h-hated him.'

'Hated him enough then to try to kill him?'

'Yes.' There, it was said. Out. No stutter or hesitation. No lingering uncertainty as the pure and dreadful force of the confession took full rein. No men had been sent down into the ravine to see if Malcolm Kerr still lived. They had not bothered because they had hoped he was dead, prayed he was dead in order to save Ginny. The awful truth of not helping a wounded man sunk in as a dreadful sin.

His laughter caught her. 'God. And you with all the talk of saving souls have tried to do away with my brother's one?'

She turned away, but he stopped her, his hand against her side. 'Nay, Grace, that was nae a criticism, only an observation of fact, and, as you did not kill him, no doubt your own soul is safe.'

'B-But it sh-should not be. I watched him f-fall and did not go to help him.'

'Was it you who pushed him over?'

When she shook her head he swore, and this time there was no humour at all in the sound. 'But you sheltered the one who did so. Why? Why did you say my brother was dead when he so plainly was not?'

Sweat was building up on her forehead, the itchy welts even itchier in her sudden emotional outburst. And outside the sound of the night encroached; a bird in the tree outside the window and the call of another further afield.

Malcolm Kerr's lips against her own as he had pulled her against him and just as quickly pushed her away. She had not meant to bite down upon his tongue, but disgust had made her react. When he had hit her across the face, she had known just exactly what sort of man he was. But she had told nobody.

Shame, she thought afterwards.

It was shame that had held her silent with her plainness and her belief that no man could truly ever be interested in her.

He had been charming the next morning to her and Stephen and her uncle. But especially to Ginny. Malcolm Kerr with his handsome face and bad temper. Everything that had happened next had been her fault, for if she had said…

'My c-cousin pushed him off his h-horse by the cliffs after h-he had tried to t-take more than she was offering.' Even the saying of it was hard, but here in a room alight with candles and the tangible feeling of safety in the glow of his eyes she wanted to tell him the truth. 'She was trying to p-push him away, just like my m-mother tried to fight before she d-died.'

'Your mother? Lord, Grace, you saw that? From the woods? When you were young?'

'And I was s-silent. I should have s-screamed. Perhaps if I had screamed he might n-not have done what he did to Mama and at G-Grantley it was the same. I knew your b-brother was dangerous, but I d-did not say so, did n-not tell them. Sh-she meant only to p-push him away, make him s-stop and she has not spoken since.'

'She was one of the girls I saw at Grantley?'

'The y-youngest one. Ginny.'

'Ginny? Ginny Sutton? GS. The notes in the jewellery box were hers, then? Not yours.' The tone in his voice was different, strident, as if her answer was important. When she nodded, he looked relieved. 'She thought sh-she loved him. She thought sh-she knew him…'

'So you pretended it was you he held the interest in?'

'I w-was twenty-five and Ginny was traumatised by it all. We felt that fewer questions would be asked this way.'

'And your cousin was what—thirteen? Fourteen?'

'Fifteen. Just.'

'Where did your uncle stand on such a pretence?'

'Behind me. He wanted Ginny p-protected. She w-was his d-daughter.'

'Whereas you were only a niece? God, what of your right to protection?'

She shook her head. 'It is n-not quite as you th-think it.'

'Then how is it, Grace? Tell me exactly how you think that it is.'

'My uncle t-took me in when my p-parents died. I was older than my cousins and n-nowhere near as p-pretty. No m-man had ever really—'

'Stop.' His fingers across her lips made her stop. 'You were expendable and it should not have been so. Did you know that your uncle had talks with my brother to marry you off to him after the battle? I heard it said at Watchlaw.'

She nodded, but stayed quiet.

'You are a beautiful woman, Grace, and you deserved a lot more care than that which you got under the guardian-ship of your uncle.'

'B-Beautiful?' The wistfulness in the word surprised even herself.

'Yes. Beautiful. To me.'

Angrily said. But no lies. He meant it. He thought that she was beautiful. To him. Warmth engulfed her in a clear rush of joy. My God, he actually meant it.

He reached forwards and took her into his arms, the warmth of his skin against her own searing away cold and with the honesty of her confessions she felt lightened, the truth between them affording a relief that was all-encompassing. And she wanted to be even closer.

With intent she unclasped the silk wrapper that Celeste had given her. Beneath it there was nothing and she waited until it pooled at her feet before looking up.

Lust sparked quick in his bleached blue eyes and for the first time in all her life Grace did indeed feel beautiful.

They lay together in the moonlight, the heady rush of lust sated and the quiet of closeness binding them into one.

Lachlan liked the way her head fitted exactly under his chin, the curly shortness of her hair tickling.

'I have not thanked you for coming to the keep at Watchlaw. We were to be hanged the next day.'

He felt her nod. So she had known it, too.

'I don't think I could have passed over a blade with more skill than you did it.'

'I had practised it many t-times in my chamber.'

He began to laugh, and thought as he did so that he had never in all his life felt this happy. Her fingers trailed light across his arm and then along the twisted scar that ran from elbow to thumb. 'How did you come by this?'

'When any royal minor ascends to any throne there is a mad scramble for power from those who would gain from it.'

'I don't understand.'

'I got in the way.'

'But this scar looks v-very old. How old were you when you "got in the way"?'

'Six. A year younger than David.'

Horror was easily heard in her voice. 'The king's enemies thought that you were him?'

'Yes.'

'Why?'

'Protection.'

'Of David.'

He nodded. 'We were of much the same age and build and my father was happy to oblige the royal minders for an undisclosed sum. When there was danger, I was dressed as him.'

'Your life for g-gold?'

'An easy exchange for everybody.'

'Except for you. You have other scars—'

His thumb covered her words, cutting them off.

'No more politics, Grace. For the moment let it just be us, aye?'

But she had not finished. 'Celeste said that you were l-lovers once?'

He threaded one hand through the darkness of his hair, the unhealed cuts on his fingers catching.

'Once, when we were bairns.' He was dismissive, as though it was something he had almost forgotten about.

'And Ruth, your first wife. What of h-her?'

'Did I love her? Is that what you are asking of me, Grace?' She nodded.

'I married her when her husband was killed. Then I was away so much that I found I could not blame her for… looking elsewhere.'

'Malcolm?' She pulled back.

'My brother always made sport of what he could not have. The child that lies in the cemetery of Belridden was theirs.'

'Lizzie said that p-people believed you poisoned Ruth…?'

When he shook his head Grace suddenly sat up. 'It was M-Malcolm, wasn't it?'

'She implied that it was so just before she died.'

'To m-more than just you?'

'She was on her death-bed and many were there to help her soul find the peace it never had in life.'

'So your brother left the k-keep and the Lairdship fell to you when it was known he was dead? But now he wants it back?'

'For a Sassenach, you are a clever wee thing.'

'Why did he wait this long to challenge you?'

'His servant was seen in London and my guess is that's where he was too. Garnering support. It would be easier to return to the Borders with an army behind his back, and if the English were offering…' He let the sentiment hang.

'Kenneth MacIndoe was the one I saw behind the tithe barn. He w-was here.'

'I thought as much.'

'But you n-never said.'

'These lands have been disputed ever since…'

'For ever.' She filled in the word as he brought her hand to his lips and kissed each finger one by one. My God, he thought as he felt her move beneath him, suggestive and eager. She was entangling him in a web. Not with Celeste, not with Ruth, not with the many other women who had warmed his bed across years of loneliness, had he felt like this. They had not smelled like Grace, nor felt like Grace nor tasted like Grace. His finger measured the pulse at her wrist and the racing beat made him smile. She did not hide her sensuality like the others, or use it to her advantage as a bargaining point, and when he had not saved her after Malcolm had kidnapped her she had come with a knife into the dungeons of Watchlaw and saved him, saved them, with monks' clothes and the waiting horses. No pouting or mop-ing or sulking either. God, that was the most refreshing thing of all. She was a woman who practised neither the deceit of guile nor the constant whine of helplessness and recrimination.

He felt the quick thud of his own heart as it tripped into a landscape it had not before ventured near. Tenderness. Attachment. Contentment.

When she opened her legs he mounted her quickly and hard, disorientated by want and desire and by the need to make her his own. For ever.

Chapter Fifteen

She had not stuttered in days, she thought as they rode into Edinburgh in the late afternoon and in the company of the King's men. Not when she was nervous or worried. Not even when the party escorting them up into Scotland had arrived at Ravenwood. She had not stuttered because Lachlan was with her, and he thought her beautiful.

They had lain together every night for the past week, cradling, needing, caught in the force of an elemental completeness. Not a little thing; breath and strength and blinded touch and secrets whispered under the cover of darkness. Lachlan understood her as no other person ever had and yet still the words that shimmered between them were unexpressed, teetering above the others of seduction and passion. Pure and honest, yet held hidden.

I. Love. You.

Simple.

Unsaid.

Tightly wound in the protection of her heart because if he did not say them back…

No. It was enough. This. It was enough to be near him, to touch him, to feel the warmth of his arms about her, protecting her, giving her a place in his life. How she hated it when the sun came up and she lost him to soldiering and intrigue and the world of men, and now to Edinburgh and his king and a court that had little liking for the English.

When her hands tightened over his he looked down, a question on his brow, but distant, as if he watched for danger even here in the city of a country he had served for ever.

He was dressed again in his Scottish clothes, the plaid today embellished with the brooch of the Kerrs, a silver stag whose points were studded with gold. His hair was plaited on each side and the rest was left long and dark, a Lord of the Marches hemmed in by small cobbled lanes. She reminded herself that he had lived in the world of courts and kings all of his life, but today he neither looked pleased nor comfortable as they wove their way up to the castle.

Edinburgh Castle was built on a huge stone rising hundreds of feet above the valley floor. Lachlan had told her of it on the way up, black rock that sealed the vent of an ancient volcano, and the sight was enthralling.

'David has asked for us to come to him.'

'Tonight?'

'Now.'

Unspoken worry surfaced.

'So soon?'

He nodded and she saw how tired he looked, his arm still

healing and his eyes reddened from the long ride. When had he last slept she wondered. Really slept? Each time at Ravenwood when she had awakened in the night he had been unsettled, the beat of his toes against the mattress suggesting a weighty problem that he dwelled upon. The king's reaction, perhaps, or his brother's betrayal? At least Duncan and Alistair and the others still alive after the battle against the English had been ransomed and were home again safely. Just one less worry in the core of all the rest.

The King greeted Lachlan effusively. He was not to be thrown in a dungeon, then, for breaking the peace against Edward. The panic that had encased her settled to a quieter distance as she stood waiting to be presented to David, King of the Scots.

He was a fair man with a full beard and an aquiline nose, the creases around his eyes suggesting laughter. On the fourth finger of his right hand he wore a wide ring, the gold burnished with the crest of the lion of Scotland, and his robes were rich.

When he turned towards her she sank into a deep curtsy and dropped her glance, surprised when he leant over and took her by the hand.

'So you are Lachlan's wife, the Stanton heiress?' he said and smiled.

'I am, your Grace.'

His smile deepened.

'Then I can well see why two men should claim you.'

'Two men?' Lachlan stepped forward, anger in his query.

'Your brother Malcolm is here. He arrived a week ago under the protection of a missive from Edward and insists that his was the prior claim to her hand.'

Silence, as each person in the room determined the consequences of such a claim.

'There is, however, a larger problem again, for Edward is displeased at your foray into England and your subsequent escape. He wants your head.'

'And you will give it to him?' Tension coated the softly said words.

'Your brother has allies in Stewart and Douglas. They too are demanding some retribution.'

'You called me back to Edinburgh to tell me this? That my brother believes he has a claim to my wife? Lord help me, if only you had sent warning…'

'You would have left. Left Belridden and Scotland, left a place that is rightfully yours.'

Grace felt in the King's words a grain of truth. Placeless. Homeless. As Lachlan had always been. Until now. She sensed the struggle in him and did not want to be the reason he would for ever after feel…stateless. When David's eyes met hers, she listened.

'Your husband has given me his life for nigh on thirty years. Now I would like to give something back to him…'

She nodded.

'I will not lose Grace.' Lachlan's words seemed strangled from very want and the grip on her hand tightened.

'And you shall not have to.' David raised his glass. 'I have suggested a tourney, a way of resolving differences here in

Edinburgh. The winner takes the Lairdship and as you and your men are the far better fighters, Lachlan, winning should be easy. Quite frankly, I was amazed that your brother even agreed to such a proposal.'

'No.' This time there was no mistaking Lachlan's intentions. 'My brother is a murderer…'

'Yet he would say that of you. He would say that your first wife Ruth was poisoned and that it was you who did it, no matter what words to the contrary were forced from her mouth in the final moments of her existence.'

'My brother loved her as I did not and she claimed to bear his child. What reason should I have for killing her when she meant so little to me?'

'Lust. Jealousy. Revenge. Malcolm was quick to name more than a few motives when I questioned him on the very same thing. He is clever, Lach, and so full of anger I would counsel caution.'

The world began to spin for Grace and she held on to the back of a high chair at her side. All this was her fault and Lachlan was in danger now because of her actions.

'How many knights?' His voice cut into her thoughts.

'Twenty each.'

'And when is this tourney to take place?'

'In two weeks.'

Standing now against the glass pane at the end of the room, her husband was silhouetted in the bright light and looked dangerous in a way she could not even begin to describe. 'Where is my brother?' A simple question with a wealth of intent placed in it.

'With Douglas, but I should warn you that many are waiting for their own chance to rule Scotland should you try to seek revenge.' He lowered his voice. 'If you take matters into your own hands, this very kingdom could totter.'

Grace thought of kingdoms and monarchs and the way politics suggested each man should sacrifice everything for the greater good. She remembered her father and mother uttering the very same words and shivered.

Lachlan felt anger reform, change and bind into a different cadence. If he took Grace and ran, they might run for ever. He felt it in the sheer temerity of his brother's demands and so far nothing had been said of Grace's lies in the whole saga. Why not? he wondered. Why had Malcolm not exposed her as a liar?

A shared guilt, probably. The yellow-haired cousin's muteness and the power of her uncle and his standing with Edward were large barriers to the truth.

David's proposal was like a gilded dagger and he could not trust in luck or skill as his king had suggested, for Malcolm was a cheat.

'I shall also name some rules of my own.' David's voice broke into his thoughts. 'You shall not meet your brother before the tourney. He shall stay in the north and you here, as my guest. Your wife will be housed with the MacDonald and his family. It is only proper.'

'Proper?' Anger filled him. Proper for him to be parted from Grace? He was amazed when he saw his wife nod.

Fourteen days. Bleakness overcame him and he nearly

refused but a small hand wormed its way into his and he knew that he could not condemn Grace to a lifetime of running.

Lady Claire MacDonald was a woman of means and morals, with a house renowned for its attention to the detail of making it safe. A good choice for Grace, but a poor one for him. There would be no visits beneath the shady cloak of darkness. The glint in David's eyes told Lachlan that he was probably thinking the very same thing.

'You'll need time between now and then to hone your skills in jousting and swordsmanship.'

The tapestried curtains opened and Lachlan knew that this meeting was at an end. Clever bastard, David. No time for arguments. He wondered if there was some sort of unseen gesture he made to his servant denoting the finish of a session. A tug on the curtain, perhaps? A stamp of the feet?

With a quick nod he turned and walked out into the company of his gathering men.

John Murray was waiting for them and he looked as unhappy as Lachlan.

'Rumour has it there is to be a tourney between you and your brother and the Lairdship of Belridden is the prize.' John Murray looked at him for confirmation, nodding as he received it. 'I'll stand with you then in the challenge, Lach. Alec and Ian could ride up from Belridden with the others. How many did he name?'

'Twenty.'

'Enough men for Malcolm to hide behind, then?'

Lachlan began to smile. 'Well, two can play at that game, aye?'

'You would kill him?'

He meant to say that he would. Meant to say it, but found that he could not quite. Malcolm was his brother and all that was left of his family. The thought was disquieting and he shook it away as the approach of a group of well-dressed women curtailed their conversation.

Grace watched him take the hand of a russet-haired woman who pressed in close.

'Alice.' He kissed the offered fingers in a manner that was so French she was taken aback. She never quite had the measure of Lachlan Kerr and he always seemed much greater than the sum of all his parts.

'Lachlan? I had heard you were in Edinburgh.' Her voice was honey warm and her smile beguiling, the gown she wore denoting both great wealth and taste.

'May I present my wife to you? Lady Grace Kerr, this is Lady Alice Drummond.'

The woman sunk into a curtsy and Grace did the same, feeling the other's eyes on the shortness of her hair. She was calculating the relationship between them, Grace thought, and seeing her as no threat at all, as an elaborately bejewelled hand threaded through Lachlan's sleeve.

'I want you to come to a banquet I am having tomorrow. And you too, John, of course. I shall expect you at around eleven in the morning. My mother will be pleased to meet you again too, Lach.'

Familiar terms, then. When her husband turned down the invite he said nothing about the conditions that the king had just exacted, nothing of her incarceration in the house of MacDonald or of his in the castle of Edinburgh.

Celeste. Alice. Ruth. Rebecca. How many other women had there been in his life? Married once, but claimed a hundred times. Looking at him here in court, she could well see why. He was beautiful in the way of a man that knew his own strength and walked his world easily, a man who carried the scars of valour and secrets in his pale blue eyes. Those eyes were at this second fastened on her in a look that was puzzled, the flat of his hand in the small of her back guiding her away from everyone and towards a doorway she had not seen before.

The room was huge, a fire burning bright in the grate and food and wine left for them on a sideboard.

Lachlan poured two generous drinks and handed her the pewter tumbler. Finishing his, he poured himself another and drank that one just as quickly before starting on a third.

'In vino veritas,' he enunciated, the amusement in his words bringing a smile to her face.

In wine there is truth.

'Shall we stay or leave, Grace? If you feel I might not win…'

She stopped him. 'If you leave, you will lose your home.'

'You are my home. Just you.'

He did not move forwards or touch her, but the air that swirled about them changed for ever. Her choice. His honesty. No lust at all involved. The candour of an unexpected confession. She could barely answer him. 'So you are saying…'

'I will go where you will it. Together.'

The muscles in the side of his jaw flexed. Not flowery prose, but enough, though it seemed to Grace that his breath was shaky. The seconds of silence stretched out. 'So if I wished to return to my holdings in England, you would follow?'

'I would.' Ground out and barely audible.

These were not the love words she had imagined in her dreams, but something much more real. He would give up even Scotland for her, a country that had marked his body during a lifetime of fighting. Tears filled her eyes. Tears not of sadness, but of wonderment, for no one ever before had given her such a gift.

'I love you, Lachlan.'

There. It was said.

'I have loved you since the first moment I saw you at Grantley and each day a little more again. But I would not take you from Belridden because the keep is your sanctuary after thirty-three years of wandering and it is mine as well.'

Home. Not just his now, but hers too. She had not realised how much she had wanted a place to call home, had not seen that, in his deliverance, came hers also.

They looked at each other, overwhelmed by the give and take of truth, but still not touching.

'If you stay with me now, Grace, I shall never let you go.'

'I know.'

'No matter how much that you should will it.'

'I know.'

Repeated. Again.

'In two minutes the door will be opened and you will be taken to the house of MacDonald.' He finished his drink and the distance between them seemed lessened. 'Promise me that you shall stay there safe. Promise me that you shall not go out alone or be swayed by any argument to leave the place, no matter who should make it…'

She moved, laying her thumb against the words and silencing worry.

'I love you, Lachlan.' The warmth of his tongue traced the line of her skin. 'You are my knight and I shall wait until you vanquish all our enemies.'

'Knight of Grace,' he whispered. 'I like that.'

'And this? Do you like this?'

She stood on tiptoes and placed her open mouth across his.

Chapter Sixteen

Grace stood still as the maids primped and plumped her hair, stood still as the gown Lady MacDonald had bequeathed her was carefully laced and the belt at her hips lain in an amber arc of citrine quartz, she supposed, or agate. She could not care which.

All her thoughts were on her husband and the last sight of him leaving her, the strange charcoal lines drawn on his wrist easily visible as his fingers had let go of her own, one by one by one.

Would he be at the court tonight? It was five whole days since she had seen him, though every night she had been taken out. Somewhere. A banquet. A dance. Each night she had looked to see if he was there and each night she was disappointed, the worry of the impending tournament weighing on her composure.

Her fault, everything, and no sign of Lachlan anywhere. And so when the servant led her into a chamber she knew to be seldom used at the bottom of the house, her heart began to beat fast. Perhaps it would be him. Here.

She stepped through the door with hope in her mouth and stopped just as suddenly. Malcolm Kerr stood watching her, his back to the fire in the hearth, his black hair highlighted by the colour of flame.

Satan. Embodied. She turned to leave.

'If you go, it will make things infinitely more difficult. I am here only to talk.' The same silky, self-serving voice then? Nothing different.

She could not believe that Lady MacDonald had meant to leave her here alone with a man whom she had much reason to hate. Unless. He seemed to know just what she was thinking as he carried on.

'Everyone in Edinburgh has secrets they wish to hide. Including your hostess.'

Blackmail and bribery. Grace stayed very still.

'If you want to protect your husband, you need to leave Edinburgh. Your being here will only be a distraction.'

'When Lachlan k-kills you?'

His smile made her nervous. Not the reaction that she might have expected.

'Such an innocent. You think it is my life that holds the key to all of this? You think that it is my continued miserable existence that I should risk everything for?'

Confusion clouded the urge to simply walk out and away. 'I don't understand.'

'Do you truly not? Then I shall endeavour to explain it to you. We are both expendable, Lachlan and I.'

'No. B-Belridden holds its own p-power.'

'Against kings?' He laughed. 'There are many landowners who are restless, Clarence is angling for a title and David still holds to the belief that Scotland can be stronger under English rule. Edward the Third would take the Marches tomorrow if he did not think that in diplomacy there is a better chance of having them anyway.'

'You w-would of course know th-that, given your own recent h-help in his campaign.'

'It is never wise to underestimate the enemy. Surely that is something you understand.'

'E-Enemy?' He spoke as if he had not thrown in his lot with the disinherited, and then she frowned when she realised it might be her family of which he spoke.

'Shifting alliances are something that an astute man can use to his own advantage.'

'Like you always h-have?'

He opened his palms in a strange gesture of intent. 'Until two weeks ago I wanted to kill you both, but today I come in peace.'

'Why? What has ch-changed?'

'My motives, I suppose. Ruth's brother told me that she took the poison herself because she wanted to punish Lachlan and me. She laid the blame upon us both and died with a smile on her face. An ague of the head, I think, from her carrying of the babe?'

Shocking, raw, the confession was so bald she could do nothing save believe it.

'Then why challenge for my hand and for Belridden? Why should you punish your brother when he did nothing to you? If you relinquished your claim, we could all go home.'

'No.' Sweat now beaded his upper lip. 'Lachlan will die unless you can find it in yourself to trust me, for you still dinna see it, do you?' Pity hung in his words. 'If I had not challenged his right to you and forced the tournament, Belridden would have become the first of the clan lands to fall into chaos, the first to be divided between two kingdoms in the name of a peaceful succession by the Duke of Clarence. A tournament highlights the right of the Kerrs to the land, makes those who might take it by subterfuge less likely to try. This way the world will see that we claim it, Lachlan and I, and that they should tread warily.'

'I d-do not know…'

'Ask your husband, then. Ask him of the king's intentions and then leave Edinburgh and go home to Grantley. Take the child that you nurture and hold it safe.'

Her hands went across the slight swell of her stomach. 'How do you know of that?'

'Your servant Lizzie has a liking for fine wine and she is not a careful drunk.' Something showed on his face, something warmer and more real.

'That was why you did not expose me, b-because of the child?'

He smiled. 'Perhaps you were not as innocent as I had thought when you made no real effort to locate my *body* at Grantley, but this babe will be the last of the Kerrs. Even a sinner has a point he tries not to cross.'

'What of your progeny? Surely you could father children?'

'Nae, I cannot.'

'But the child Ruth bore?'

'Wasn't mine.'

'Lachlan insists that she was n-not his either, yet he buried the child in consecrated ground and cursed you for it as he did so.' The facts fell bare between them and Grace ran her hands through the short length of her hair. Lord, what was she to do now? Candour had its own barbed points and she could see in Malcolm Kerr's eyes the beginning of comprehension.

Not his? Not his brother's? The woman he loved obviously had had her own demons.

His face reddened and his teeth gripped at his upper lip. For a second she thought that he might cry in front of her, the bullish cocksure man of a minute ago submerged under a mask of grief.

Lord, Grace thought. So here was the truth. A family pulled apart by death, curses and poison and a woman too weak to see her part in the healing.

Still she could not absolve him of everything.

'Ginny, my cousin…'

'She said she wanted me. I thought that she was saying yes.'

Another truth. And perhaps her cousin had wanted him. The letters. The meetings. Complex and startling, and just like that, the man who had been a puzzle became one who was not.

'I sh-should have sent men to look for you. I sh-should have tried harder, but I w-was angry.'

He made no comment at all to that.

'I've made many mistakes in my life. One of them was trusting Ruth and another was throwing my lot in with the English. But at the very end of it all, Belridden stands as the only true thing that matters, the real treasure that needs to be saved. We can only do that if Lachlan and I take on those against us and win, for otherwise it will be lost to the Kerrs.'

'Cross the f-field, you mean, with everyone l-looking on?'

He nodded. 'It could work if none could guess that I planned to do it. Is it possible for you to see my brother before the tournament?'

'I am n-not certain. So far I have n-not.'

'He won't trust my intentions.'

'Can you b-blame him for that?'

'Tell him first if you see him. Tell him it is for the name of Kerr that I am fighting and for the babe you carry—'

'He does not know of this child,' she butted in. 'I have not had the chance to say it.'

His smile surprised her as it made him look so much more like her husband. 'Lachlan protected a child he thought was mine. It is the least I can do to protect one that I know is his.'

A noise outside made them turn and Claire MacDonald entered the room, her pallor deathly white and her hands trembling. She looked straight at Grace and crossed the floor to stand by her.

She was a good woman with difficult choices and the fibre within to make the right one. Malcolm could learn a lot from her.

As if he had had the same thought he turned to leave, his silence allowing the woman at least some comfort, and when the tapestried curtain hung down behind him and there was stillness, Claire burst into copious tears.

'If he hurt you in any way…'

'He did not.' Grace took the cold hands into her own, liking the way the fingers threaded through hers. 'And he will not hurt you or your family either.'

A glimmer of relief was followed by even louder sobs as Lady MacDonald realised how close she had come to losing everything she held dear.

Grace saw her husband later that night from a distance, his hair slicked close and a shirt and plaid showing off the dark of his skin. He was like an outsider caught here among the fine clothes and manners, and, for the first time she could ever remember, he did not carry a weapon within the company of others. His choice, or the wish of those near him, she knew not which, though the beat of his fingers against the emptiness of his belt gave her some sort of an idea, as did the presence of men she had not met before. He was being as watched as she was.

She tried to compose herself, tried to swallow back panic as he walked across the room towards her. Even dressed in the finery Claire had lent her, she was…ordinary compared to him…the beauty she had perceived a few hours ago in front of her mirror less certain here.

'Grace.'

He said her name softly as he took her hand. No more than that, just the feel of his skin against her own. For a moment she did not meet his eyes, could not, could not look and see what she hoped was there. And then she did, there in the middle of a crowded room with the lights of the candles above them and outside the Scottish autumn settling close.

His fingers tightened, the ball of his thumb running across the sensitive flesh inside her palm, promising all the things that they might do later. Much later, with politics and the way of the court now binding them to different paths.

When he stepped back their hands fell away, his smile bright. She could see other women watching him, prettier women than she and cleverer. Still he stayed there, close.

'Ye have been well?'

'I have been, my Lord.' So polite in this company as manners stripped the words of meaning. 'And you?'

'Well.' The glint in his eyes bordered on humorous, though danger was imprinted there too, and, as John Murray wove his way through the crowd, new hope surfaced.

'I wish to have a moment alone with the Kerrs,' he ordered and unexpectedly took her arm as he moved with Lachlan away towards the window, shepherding them to the least used part of the room.

'We have a minute at most, Grace,' her husband said as they walked. 'By then they will have realised that John here has no mandate at all to dictate their behaviour.'

'Who are they?' she asked.

'Men from the north! David is under threat from everybody these days and so he lets them have their head.'

'I have met your brother.' She rushed the words out, and she was glad that he had not tried to touch her as the distraction would muddle her thoughts and she needed to tell him. 'He knows that I carry your child.'

'Wha-a-at?' Even John Murray turned around at that.

'I know this is a t-terrible place and time to t-tell you, Lachlan, but it makes a difference to why Malcolm will help us.'

'You are with child?'

'What difference?'

Two questions from two men. She answered the one of her husband.

'By almost eight weeks.'

'And you are well?' His hand came across the swell of her stomach, carefully, as if even the gentlest of touches might disturb the baby.

'Your brother says that he will cross the field at the tournament and support you. He says that Belridden is in danger of being divided up between all those who would support David and that Edward of England is losing patience. He says that the Kerr land will be the first to be sacrificed to appease the English monarch.'

'Have you heard these rumours?' Lachlan looked to John for confirmation, but Murray shrugged his shoulders.

'The envoy from Edward came to Edinburgh with your brother. It is anyone's guess what was talked of.'

'So it could be true?'

'Aye, it could be. Edward has made no secret of the fact that he supports those stripped of their lands under the Bruce.'

'Lord, Grace, you need to get out of Edinburgh and go back to Grantley.'

'No. You need to win at the tournament, and when you do we will ride back to Belridden.'

'Listen to me—if you love me you will listen to me, Malcolm is not to be trusted…'

But the time was up and before she could even give an answer, her husband was bustled away and out of the room.

John Murray still stood beside her.

'In your reasoning, why should we now trust Lach's brother?'

'Because we have to,' she answered back, less and less sure of her motives in the wake of her husband's advice. If Malcolm Kerr betrayed them now, it would be more dangerous than before. At least then Lachlan would have been ready for him, but behind his back…

She shook her head and refused to even think about it.

Lachlan walked back to his rooms alone.

Grace was having their child. Conceived when? His mind ran back over the weeks.

The first time he had gone to her room perhaps? The thought amazed him. Would it be a lad or a lassie with hair the colour of the rowanberries in full blush? Would she be safe, they be safe? She had looked tired and uncertain, the dress a full size too big. Not her own, then. Lady MacDonald's, perhaps, or one of her grown up daughters? He noticed too that his ring on her finger was still loose and that she wore the clip from Constantinople he had bought her.

He loved her. Loved her as he had never loved anyone before, because with love came risk and loss. He could see now why his father took refuge in drink after his mother had died.

And she had died in childbirth, too. His heart began to pound. She was small like his mother. What if it should claim her life as well? How would he live? And why would she not go to Grantley, to safety, the power of the Carrick name protecting her there like his own could not here? He had seen the same look in her eyes in court as he had in the cells of the Watchlaw Castle. Forceful. Certain. What was she up to? Where had she seen Malcolm and why should he now take the leap into brotherhood when in the years of their growing up he had not?

No. That was not quite true. There had been a time when Malcolm and he had been friends, good friends, between the constant journeying to David and the growing bitterness of their father. Even after that, he thought. When Hugh had been buried they had forged the old bonds back. For a while. It was only recently his brother had been fully lost to him over the saga of Ruth. Guilt rose. Perhaps his brother had loved her as he had not? Perhaps now knowing what he did about love and feelings he might have acted differently, not having then understood what drew people together and what tore them apart.

Ruth! People had said that she had not been happy for a long while, as long as their marriage had lasted perhaps, two people bound by nothing save a troth.

He had not known then what could bind lovers, the white-hot strands of joy and passion foreign to him. He had not understood that his indifference to her suffering might have cut like a quick into the heightened feelings of his brother.

Love. It had come unexpectedly, like a flash flood in the

hills behind Belridden in the early fullness of spring or the hailstorms bearing down from the Cheviots when winter blanketed the Eastern Marches. Unstoppable. Elemental. Grace.

In court today she had looked magnificent, no other word for it, and though there were woman more beautiful in the conventional sense or more shapely, it was to Grace that his glance kept returning, her bravery worn like a banner.

She believed in the power of good. She believed that a solution to the struggle in the Borderlands could be achieved and that he was the man to do it. Aye, and she did not falter under her beliefs either or wear a paltry timidity. Faint-hearted and fearful? How could he have ever thought her such?

But would this plan work?

Lord. He swiped back his hair and leaned against the cold stone behind him. He wanted to see his child grow up, wanted to be the sort of father to it that his own had not been to him, wanted Belridden to ring again with the sound of laughter and hope. Perhaps all this could be possible again? Perhaps in the next generations of Kerrs, peace, prosperity and trust might come again to the keep?

Because of Grace.

'Mother of Mary, let that be so,' he whispered to himself, and tried to imagine what his child's face might look like.

Chapter Seventeen

The tourney was held in a field outside Edinburgh, the list measuring three hundred yards by a hundred and with no rules as to the allowed number of blows. From a stand behind a double-barrier fence Grace watched the fluttering banners and coats-of-arms, the colourful pageantry belying the danger involved. She had never in her entire life seen such a spectacle, the canopied and tiered stands decorated with shields of a hundred colours and more than a thousand people watching, peasants and nobles alike, all caught up in the excitement of the event. Like a sport!

Claire MacDonald took her hand and squeezed. 'I am certain that your husband will be safe, and win the challenge.' Grace thought her quavery voice belied the inherent message in it, but any answer was drowned out by a fanfare of eight trumpeters announcing the arrival of David, King of the Scots, accompanied by his highborn nobles. Today he looked every inch the head of a royal lineage, and when he caught Grace's eye she curtsied in respect. His allegiances were complicated and this challenge under the guise of Malcolm Kerr's revenge must have caused him many a sleepless night. But her husband was the King's man after all and she needed the monarch to believe that the loyal support he had from the Laird of Kerr was enough. Enough to let them retire back to the Belridden stronghold after the tournament and into a relative obscurity. Lord, how she hoped so.

Another worm of worry turned in her stomach, etching away her capacity to reason properly. Malcolm said he had delivered his letter of challenge to protect Belridden, but with the tourney about to start she wondered if it was a ruse after all. Could he be trusted? Her fingers twisted Lachlan's gold ring as she pondered on what might happen should her husband lose this contest. Knights died in such battles and women were widowed.

The horror of the thought made her skin prickle. Lord, the itchiness that she had been plagued with when first she had left Grantley was back and the rash on her forearms seemed to be reddening with each passing second.

No. She could not let fear take away her trust. Malcolm Kerr would keep to his word and her husband was reputed to be the finest fighter in all of Scotland. Sitting up straighter, she plastered a smile across abject terror and stilled her hands as they twisted the fabric in her red-and-green brocade skirt.

The packed galleries had quietened as the trumpets played and the knights led by their retainers came into sight, each hoisting aloft their particular coat of arms on sturdy wooden stakes. Red, gold, black, purple and green, the tinctures of badges and fields and standards fluttered and the bards and shaffrons covering the horses swirled. Lachlan appeared first, the red and green of his family colours proclaiming for all to see his right to the Belridden land, and Grace's heart, already pumping, began to beat louder. Cheering echoed around the arena and the other ladies of court sat forwards on their ornate wooden chairs.

Lachlan Kerr was the favourite, and, with hair flowing and pale eyes perusing the galleries without a hint of concern, she could well see why. His armour was unlike any of the others. Tarnished and well worn, its smooth planes altered into an unevenness denoting other battles. Not the tournaments, Grace thought, for he had not taken part in those, but the true and real jeopardy of war. She breathed in, the strength of love and worry like a pain in her throat.

Tilting his lance, her husband walked his steed up to the first barrier some thirty feet from where she sat and the world slowed and quietened. Just her and just him, separated by the distance of risk and danger. The mantling on the crest of his helmet was nowhere near as ornate or fussy as the others behind him and his shoulders were broad and straight.

She had a sudden vision of him falling, a dagger thrust through the vision-slit of his visor, blood running crimson across the lighter red and green. No. Not him. Not now. Her hand lay across the swell of her stomach even as he turned to line up at one end of the field.

Lord, this was it!

The moment she had been dreading was here and she had heard that there was little chivalry in tournaments. Knights ganged up on other knights and the daggers hidden on their personage were carefully used in the less protected areas of an opponent's body, the parts where the rivets and straps of leather provided a lesser barrier and where a sharp blade might do the maximum of damage.

A lone rider in red and green bursting from the entrance way brought her attention back to the field, his colours matching her husband's exactly, as noise hushed into puzzlement and query. Even David leaned forwards to watch as Malcolm Kerr cantered across to stop at the right-hand side of his brother.

All looked to the King. Would he halt the tourney, deeming the rules broken? The mounting shouts of the crowd suggested anger should the spectacle not be allowed and when the king's messenger signalled for two of the re-tainers behind Lachlan to drop away, relief settled.

Nineteen men against nineteen men, lances and swords at the ready and polished metal gleaming in the daylight.

A single man walked across to the barrier with his flag down and all those in armour settled their lances. When the flag came up they charged, clods of earth flying and dust swirling as the drumming noise of hooves came closer, closer and closer.

Every other knight on that field lifted their chin at the last moment before contact was made, to protect their eyes, Grace supposed, but leaving them vulnerable in the seeing of the target. Everyone that was except for her husband and his lance splintered against his opponent's chest dead in the centre, whipping the man's body back and off his horse in one clean movement. A great cheer resounded as Lachlan thundered by, reeling his horse in at the far end of the field, the steed turning effortlessly, guided by experience and expertise, the line of his body melded with that of his mount, balanced on a knife edge. As he signalled his men to wait, there seemed no question in Lachlan's stance that they would follow and win. Already on the field two of the opposition had fallen, the attendants rushing in to drag them to the safety afforded by the fences.

New lances were brought out and the flag fell again, Malcolm Kerr shadowing his brother as they charged, the lances exploding into shards of wood on contact, though this time the knights did not retreat, but stayed locked together in a closer battle. Swords were unsheathed and mounts whinnied and reared, the destrier of Lachlan's the steadiest. Perhaps the big black horse had travelled in France under the banner of Philip or in England under Edward to make him so placid in a time of battle. Grace could no longer think because in the mêlée Lachlan had been isolated, the opposition steeds providing a barrier against his own men.

She stood on her feet and screamed at him to get away, the words whipped to nothing, the arched circular stands awash with people craning their necks, cheering, mere diversion and sport and a way to pass the time. Not for her, though, not for her. If he should fall here and if she should lose him…

Lachlan cursed as a blade found its way beneath the protection afforded by his mail aventail. Kicking out at the flanks of the horse holding the rider, he was rewarded by a clear view of his opponent's armpit and took his chance.

The scream of pain drew the others and for a moment he was caught by a solid wall of horse and armour, a barrier to the help of his retainers as the opposition gave it their best to try to kill him. He felt the pain in his side only as a small pinch and when he tried to raise his left arm he found he could not. With care he transferred his sword to his other hand and pushed at those that held him, fighting to find distance and space. Many Kerrs were left-handed, but he had always been ambidextrous and today the fact stood him in good stead. The toppling of two of the enemy gave him hope and he kicked through, breaking loose as Malcolm slashed behind him.

'Double back,' he shouted to his brother, the battle-cry of the Kerrs sounding in the mêlée.

'Belleden. Belleden.'

They made easy work of two knights caught on their horses at an unfavourable position. Lachlan doubted that they had even known what had hit them as they fell and lay still.

Eight down now, though his own men had fallen too. Andrew and Ian and Alec. Rob was next to him and Malcolm, and further away Stuart fought.

In the heat of the battle Lachlan forgot the crowd and the field and his king. But not Grace. He did not forget her. She'd called out a warning to him at one time, her green dress with the red bands like a beacon to his eyes as his left side ached and damned men kept coming at him.

There were twelve of them left now, nine on the other side and only Malcolm, Stuart and him on this one. He stayed near his brother, liking the feel of him at his back, a kind of elation filling him ever since he had seen him break from the entrance in the colours of the Kerrs and cross the field. Not all lies, then. Not all betrayal.

Malcolm went down suddenly, the angle of his fall worrying and his stillness even more so. Lachlan fought for control as the hooves of his horse missed his head by a whisker, Zeus prancing sidewards from the jab of a knife aimed at him. Honour was as lost on this field as it never was in war, Lachlan thought, as he turned and sheltered his brother, the fence a welcome block, a way at least of buying time until an attendant came to get him. But something was not right in the gurgle of Malcolm's breath and the bright red blood that seeped from his aventail on to the dust below.

Whipping up his visor, Lachlan slid from his horse, whistling to Zeus to stay exactly where he was. He had his brother's helmet off in a second and the damage to his throat was as startling as the tears that ran down his cheek.

'I tried, Lach. I tried to help…'

'You did help.' His sword parried as a rider who had come in behind on foot leapt at them. Without any hesitation, Lachlan ran the point through the opened slit of his helmet. He stood for the next one, hard anger making short work of him too. No one could have touched him on that field, no one could have got to his brother. It was for Malcolm he now fought, for the good times and the bad ones, for the years when they had been siblings in the true sense of the word, before Dalbeth's prophecy and his mother's death, before Hugh's drinking problems and the way that war had torn out the heart of every family along the border.

When he saw that Stuart had managed to garner the attention of the remaining knights, he brought his brother across his knee, discarding his gauntlets and wiping away the blood, feeling as he did so the growing coldness in Malcolm's skin.

'God forgive me…my sins, Lachy.' His childhood name! He swallowed.

'He will, I am certain of it, aye.'

'And you. Do you forgive me?'

He nodded his head. 'Ahhh, Malcolm, *sero sed serio…* late but in earnest.'

But he was gone from this earth, the glazed stillness of his eyes widening as his soul disappeared. Gone. For ever. He held him close before laying him down and standing. Five knights left against just Stuart and himself. Anger coursed through him and a fatalism that hardened everything.

Removing his visor completely, he stepped into the ring of men and began to fight.

Something was not right. Malcolm was not moving and Lachlan was favouring his left side. And yet the way he fought was unlike anything Grace had ever seen before, no face protection now, his helmet and gauntlets lying by his fallen brother, his hair dark-wet against the matt of his worn armour and his sword slashing. Two left now and then one. Stuart took no part in the spectacle as her husband finished off the last remaining resistance. Easily.

And then went down on his knees and lifted up his

brother, cradling the limp form in an embrace that was both fiercely protective and undeniably private even in that arena of a thousand men and women, the blood on his cheek swiped away in a gesture that defied pity and mirrored the sort of fury that only heroes might finally feel.

The echo of his name began as a single voice in the gallery of the peasants, Grace was to think later, a quiet acknowledgment to bravery. And then it grew. 'Lachlan Kerr, Laird of the Marches', echoing around the stands, accolades of a new legend and the deeds that bards and jesters might recall and retell down through the coming of the next generations. Honour. Prowess. Respect. Two brothers caught in the clash of ideas and holding true to the Declaration of Arbroath through life and death. *'For we fight not for glory, nor riches, nor honours, but for freedom alone which no good man gives up except with his life.'*

And it had been given, here, today, in the blood of the Kerrs, their colours slashed with crimson and dust and the tears of a seasoned knight who would cry before them all after fighting them all.

Grace's own eyes welled and she stood, running, running to her husband, the ache in her throat growing as she came closer.

He caught her to him, the warmth of her skin, the tears on her face and her flame-coloured hair, his woman, his wife, beautiful in a way no other woman would ever be, her simple honesty shining bright.

'I love you, *mo chride*.' Easily said. Nothing held back.

'I love you, too.'

His fingers threaded through her hair, but they did not kiss. Not here. Not in this arena. That would come later.

'Malcolm's dead.' He hated the catch in his voice.

'He died for you and for Belridden.'

'I know.'

The trumpets sounded again, and the cheering was untempered as David walked on to the field.

Lachlan bowed his head, but David caught his arm and held it high, turning him so that he could be seen from all the stands and vantage points. Favours were thrown, fluttering down from the higher tiers and the lower ones until the earth was a sea of colour. He saw Grace pick up one in the shades of red and green and bring it to her breast, but David was speaking now and the crowds quietened.

'I say that Lachlan Kerr, the Laird of Belridden, shall hold the Eastern Marches safe for Scotland.'

Lachlan got an impression of his liege using the moment for his own gains and he smiled. Perhaps this country was in safer hands than he had thought, the threat of the northern landowners and of the English receding a little. Perhaps Malcolm's death *had* meant something, *had* changed something, *had* melded a land splintered and greedy into something better.

He hoped so even as he reached for Grace.

The wound was far worse than he had let her see, she thought twenty minutes later as Lachlan's squires pulled back the padded linen of his tunic. All across the back of his neck and the folds of skin on his upper arms blood welled, but it was the deeper gash beneath his left arm that was the most worrying. Grace saw the beaded sweat rise on his forehead as the young servant dabbed at the blood with a wet cloth.

'It is deep,' she ventured, but he stopped her.

'Believe me, I have had far worse than this and lived.'

'In battle?'

'And away from it.'

In the light of the tent with his chest bare, Grace could easily see the traces of many other wounds, scars now whitened by time. Not just a few, but many; taking his hand in her own, she brought his fingers to her lips, kissing each one by one.

'Will this be the end of it?'

He smiled and nodded and she thought that his strength and certainty would forever keep her safe.

'Thanks to Malcolm it will be.'

On another pallet with his hands folded across his breast Malcolm Kerr lay, his dagger gleaming and clean in his fingers, as though even in death he might still fight.

The noise of the crowd outside filtered louder through the thin canvas of their tent, and as the flaps were folded back Grace frowned. Already the space was filled with well-wishers and all she wanted was the chance to tend to her husband herself.

A large black dog bounded in unfettered and leapt at them both.

'Dexter?' She bent to his warm wet kisses and laughed out loud, her fingers searching out his body for the wounds she had seen there last time. Nothing remained, and when Lachlan put out his hand she let him go, marvelling that a dog of his size would sense the need for care. He did not jump at Lachlan as he had with her, but nuzzled into his hand, sitting on his haunches by the pallet and staying still.

'How did he come here?' Grace had her answer a second later when her uncle and three cousins appeared, their faces filled with concern. Connor Kerr limped in behind them, his wide smile at Grace's gasp of surprise suggesting a man returned to almost full health. Her husband's Gaelic greeting was warm, another friend restored to them in the calmness between political upheavals.

Her uncle, however, was not to be left waiting, pushing into the space with all the energy of a man half his age. 'We had a missive arrive at Grantley from a John Murray informing us that we were needed in Edinburgh and so went by way of Belridden. This dog insisted on following us from your keep and five miles out we decided to let him in and bring him to you both.'

The sudden gasp of Ginny made everyone turn.

'Malcolm.' Torn from anguish and disbelief and agony, the small bag that she carried dropped as she rushed to his side and threw herself across him.

The first word she had uttered on nigh on a year was not to be her last. 'I thought I had killed him! I thought he had died at Grantley?'

'Nay, Ginny, he lived. He came to help, to help us here, to fight in the tournament.'

'I thought it was my fault…I thought it was all my fault that he died…'

'Shh.' Grace held her cousin still, the many ears listening dangerous to a carelessly offered confession, and Judith, understanding the predicament, walked forwards to shepherd her sister from the tent.

Her uncle turned back to Lachlan. 'It seems we have much to apologise for and thank you for. Grace is happy. I can see it in her eyes and hear it in her voice. You do not stammer any more, niece?'

'No.' On reflection it had been a while since she had.

'And your skin condition is so much improved.'

'It is.'

'We are having a child in the summer.' Lach's words were proudly said and Dexter barked as if he too sent felicitations, making everyone laugh.

A new beginning then. A new heir for Belridden and for lands that were now so much more secure. And Malcolm would be buried there. For ever there. Another fallen son of the keep of Belridden claimed as a hero in death.

She prayed to God that peace might now rule the Borderlands.

Epilogue

All candles were snuffed out save for one as the winds from the mountains hurled themselves against the ramparts of Belridden. But inside they were warm, tucked beneath fine skins of deer on a bed of feather softness.

Safety. How she loved it. Her finger touched the cheek of her husband, the new ring he had given her glinting in what little was left of the light.

'In my childhood dreams you looked exactly the same as you do right now, at this moment.'

He laughed at that and traced a line across the tilt of her nose. 'When your mother named you Grace she chose the right name.'

'How so?' she teased him, hearing the laughter in her question, but he did not return it, his voice as serious as she had ever heard.

'Because grace has finally come to me and without you…' He did not finish as her tongue ran around the sensitive skin on the inside of his thumb.

'Love me,' he whispered and turned to cover her body

with his own, the wound on his side much healed in the three days it had taken to journey to Belridden. He was careful with his weight upon her, settling his hands at her hips.

'I would nae wish to hurt the bairn, but I need you close, like this.' His knees opened her legs and she opened them further, holding him to her, warm and right.

'When you told me you loved me on the field at Edinburgh…?' He had not said it again.

'I love you, *mo nighean mhaiseach,* and will do so for ever. I swear it.'

The pale eyes caught in the light of the single candle were shadow-blue. Beautiful. Like the first time she had ever seen him, as he had strode into Grantley. But now the beauty did not worry her and he was not disappointed. She could see that in the way his eyes widened as she reached out and offered him everything.

* * * * *

HISTORICAL

Novels coming in January 2009

THE RAKE'S DEFIANT MISTRESS
Mary Brendan

Snowbound with notorious rake Sir Clayton Powell,
defiant Ruth Hayden manages to resist falling into
his arms. But Clayton hides the pain of past betrayal
behind his charm, and even Ruth, no stranger to scandal,
is shocked by the vicious gossip about him. Recklessly,
she seeks to silence his critics – by announcing
their engagement…

THE VISCOUNT CLAIMS HIS BRIDE
Bronwyn Scott

Viscount Valerian Inglemoore has been a secret agent on
the war-torn Continent for years. Now he has returned for
Philippa Stratten – the woman he was forced to leave behind.
But Philippa, deeply hurt by his rejection, is unwilling to
risk her heart again. Valerian realises he'll have to fight
a fiercer battle to win her as his bride…

THE MAJOR AND
THE COUNTRY MISS
Dorothy Elbury

Returning hero Major William Maitland finds himself
tasked with the strangest mission – hunting down the lost
heir to his uncle's fortune. While searching in Warwickshire
for the twenty-year-old secret he meets the beautiful but
secretive Georgianne Venables, who may prove to be his
personal Waterloo…

**Another exciting novel
available this month is:**

MARRYING THE MISTRESS

Juliet Landon

Guardian . . . and husband

Helene Follet hasn't had close contact with
Lord Burl Winterson since she chose to spend her
life caring for his brother. Now she's forced to live
under Burl's protection, because he has become
guardian to her precious young son.

Burl has grown hard and cynical over the years, while
Helene covers her hurt with an ice-cool front. What she
really craves is to finally find a loving home in his safe,
strong arms. Neither can admit that they are still
tantalised by the memory of one magical, fateful night…